Thomas Middleton's A Chaste Maid in Cheapside: A Retelling

David Bruce

Published by David Bruce, 2023.

THOMAS MIDDLETON'S A CHASTE MAID IN CHEAPSIDE: A RETELLING

First edition. March 21, 2023.

ISBN: 979-8201520717

Written by David Bruce.

Table of Contents

Dedication

DEDICATED TO MY SISTER MARTHA

Martha wrote, "When I was working at Longaberger, I worked with a girl who had two children and was in the middle of a divorce. She was so worried about Christmas for her boys. I received a very nice Christmas bonus that year, and I went to my boss and started a donation fund for the girl. My boss told me later that she — my boss — delivered the money to the girl's mother and father and told them not to tell her who brought the money for her. Months later the girl told me that the boys had the best Christmas that year, and she told me someone had brought money to her mom and dad for her, and she went to town and bought the boys Christmas. She never did know who did that for her. She was so thankful. I believe that I was the only one who donated to her, which was just fine."

***

The doing of good deeds is important. As a free person, you can choose to live your life as a good person or as a bad person. To be a good person, do good deeds. To be a bad person, do bad deeds. If you do good deeds, you will become good. If you do bad deeds, you will become bad. To become the person you want to be, act as if you already are that kind of person. Each of us chooses what kind of person we will become. To become a good person, do the things a good person does. To become a bad person, do the things a bad person does. The opportunity to take action to become the kind of person you want to be is yours.

Bai Juyi went to Zen master Daolin of the Tang Dynasty and asked what one must do in order to live in accord with the Tao. Daolin answered, "One must avoid doing evil, and one must do as much good as possible." Bai Juyi was surprised at the simplicity of this answer and said, "Even a child knows that." "True," replied Daolin, "even a child of three knows this but even a man of 80 fails to live up to it."

A seeker after truth once asked a wise person how to seek God. The wise person replied, "The ways to God are as many as there are created beings. But the shortest and easiest is to serve others, not to bother others, and to make others happy."

The Zen master Gisan was taking a bath. The water was too hot, so he asked a student to add some cold water to the bath. The student brought a bucket of cold water, added some cold water to the bath, and then threw the rest of the water on a rocky path. Gisan scolded the student: "Everything can be used. Why did you waste the rest of the water by pouring it on the path? There are some plants nearby which could have used the water. What right do you have to waste even a drop of water?" The student became enlightened and changed his name to Tekisui, which means "Drop of Water."

Educate Yourself
Read Like A Wolf Eats
Be Excellent to Each Other
Books Then, Books Now, Books Forever

***

In this retelling, as in all my retellings, I have tried to make the work of literature accessible to modern readers who may lack some of the knowledge about mythology, religion, and history that the literary work's contemporary audience had.

Do you know a language other than English? If you do, I give you permission to translate this book, copyright your translation, publish or self-publish it, and keep all the royalties for yourself. (Do give me credit, of course, for the original retelling.)

I would like to see my retellings of classic literature used in schools, so I give permission to the country of Finland (and all other countries) to give copies of this book to all students forever. I also give permission to the state of Texas (and all other states) to give copies of this book to all students forever. I also give permission to all teachers to give copies of this book to all students forever.

Teachers need not actually teach my retellings. Teachers are welcome to give students copies of my books as background material. For example, if they are teaching Homer's *Iliad* and *Odyssey*, teachers are welcome to give students copies of my *Virgil's* Aeneid: *A Retelling in Prose* and tell students, "Here's another ancient epic you may want to read in your spare time."

CAST OF CHARACTERS

Mr. YELLOWHAMMER, a goldsmith.

MAUDLIN, his wife.

TIM, their son.

MOLL, their daughter. "Moll" is a nickname for "Mary." A "moll" can be a prostitute. "Mary" calls to mind the Virgin Mary.

TUTOR to Tim.

SIR WALTER Whorehound, a suitor to Moll.

SIR OLIVER Kix, and his wife LADY KIX, kin to Sir Walter.

ALLWIT, and his wife MISTRESS ALLWIT, whom Sir Walter keeps — that is, provides for.

A WELSH GENTLEWOMAN, Sir Walter's whore.

WAT and NICK, Sir Walter's bastards by Mistress Allwit.

DAVY Dahumma, Sir Walter's serving-man. "Dahumma" means "Come here" in this phonetic version of Welsh.

TOUCHWOOD SENIOR, a decayed — with reduced financial assets — gentleman.

His wife MISTRESS TOUCHWOOD.

TOUCHWOOD JUNIOR, another suitor to Moll. A younger brother to Touchwood Senior.

TWO PROMOTERS. Promoters are informers.

SERVANTS, three of Allwit's, three of Sir Oliver's.

Three or four WATERMEN. Watermen ferry passengers across the Thames River.

Sims, a PORTER.

A GENTLEMAN.

A WENCH with Touchwood Senior's bastard.

Jugg, Lady Kix' MAID.

A DRY NURSE.

A WET NURSE. A wet nurse breastfeeds infants.

A MAN with a basket.

A SECOND MAN with a basket.

TWO PURITANS, the first named Mistress Underman.

FIVE GOSSIPS. Gossips are 1) godparents, or 2) female friends. Gossips can be friends invited to witness the christening of a newborn.

A MIDWIFE.

A PARSON.

A third NURSE.

SUSAN, Moll's chambermaid.

SCENE: London

NOTES:

"A chaste maid" is 1) a chased maiden, and 2) a sexually chaste maiden.

A maid is a maiden: 1) a young unmarried woman, and/or 2) a virgin.

A maid can also be a servant.

Cheapside, aka Westcheap, is a street on which many goldsmiths' shops were located. It ran from St. Paul's Cathedral to the Poultry. Goldsmiths' Row was located in the south of Cheapside. Prostitutes were punished by being whipped along its length.

"Yellowhammer" is Elizabethan and Jacobean slang for "gold coin." A "yellowhammer" is also a chattering bird.

"Maudlin" is how "Maudline" was pronounced. "Maudline" is Mary "Magdalene," a reformed prostitute in the Bible.

"Allwit" is word play on "wittol," which means "complacent cuckold."

The Latin is often garbled in this play. This may be done intentionally for comic effect, or it may be the result of faulty transcription. Some editors correct the Latin; some don't.

The Welsh in this play is phonetic, and its meaning is often unclear. This was and is not a problem because chances are, few people in the audience then or now understood or understand Welsh.

Playwrights at this time were very bawdy. Knowing that, people today may find bawdiness that the playwright did not intend. This may happen in this retelling. A reviewer on an online bookseller compared me (David Bruce) to a sniggering schoolboy who looks up "dirty" words in the dictionary.

In this society, a person of higher rank would use "thou," "thee," "thine," and "thy" when referring to a person of lower rank. (These terms were also used affectionately and between equals.) A person of lower rank would use "you" and "your" when referring to a person of higher rank.

"Sirrah" was a title used to address someone of a social rank inferior to the speaker. Friends, however, could use it to refer to each other.

The word "wench" at this time was not necessarily negative. It was often used affectionately.

CHAPTER 1
— 1.1 —

Maudlin and Moll talked together in front of Yellowhammer's shop in Cheapside. Yellowhammer was a goldsmith, and Maudlin and Moll were his wife and daughter.

Maudlin asked her daughter, "Have you played over all your old lessons on the virginals?"

The virginals were a keyboard instrument.

"Yes," Moll replied.

Maudlin said:

"Yes, you are a dull maiden recently. I think you need to have something to quicken your greensickness."

A maiden is a virgin.

Greensickness is actually a form of anemia suffered by many young girls at the time when they started menstruating. People at the time believed, however, that greensickness was a form of lovesickness, and the cure for greensickness was to get a husband.

"Quicken" means "revive," or "become pregnant."

Maudlin continued:

"Do you weep? A husband. Had not such a piece of flesh been ordained, what had we wives been good for?"

The piece of flesh is a penis.

Maudlin continued:

"To make salads, or else cried up and down for samphire."

Salads are green, and a maiden suffering from greensickness had a greenish tint.

Salads were seasoned.

"Samphire" was the name given to two plants. One was used in salads; the other was pickled and eaten with meat.

"To make salads" can mean "to become salads." Something "cried up and down" is for sale. If a husband is a piece of meat, and if a wife is a salad, then the two together make a satisfying meal.

Maudlin continued:

"To see the difference of these seasons!"

"To see the difference of these seasons!" can mean "How times have changed!" Or it can mean "These seasonings are different."

Maudlin continued:

"When I was of your youth, I was lightsome, and quick, two years before I was married."

The word "quick" can mean 1) high-spirited, and/or 2) pregnant.

Maudlin continued:

"You fit for a knight's bed — drowsy-browed, dull-eyed, drossy-spirited! I bet my life that you have forgotten your dancing — when was the dance teacher with you?"

"Last week," Moll said.

Maudlin said:

"Last week? When I was of your bord, he missed me not a night — I was kept at it."

When Maudlin said, "When I was of your bord," she meant, "When I was like you."

"Bord" means "bore." The bore of a gun is the size of the barrel the bullet travels through.

Maudlin's words were unintentionally bawdy. "Dancing" can mean "having sex," as does "kept at it." "Bord" can refer to vaginal size.

"Bord" may, however, mean "board." Then Maudlin would mean when she was still living with her parents, the way that Moll is doing now.

Maudlin continued:

"I took delight to learn, and he to teach me. Pretty brown and dark-complexioned gentleman, he took pleasure in my company, but you are dull. Nothing comes nimbly from you, you dance like a plumber's daughter, and you deserve two thousand pounds in lead to your marriage, and not in goldsmith's ware."

Plumbers used lead in their work, and so people might joke that a plumber's daughter was leaden-footed while dancing.

Yellowhammer entered the scene.

He asked, "Now what's the din — quarrel — between mother and daughter, huh?"

"Indeed, a small din," Maudlin said. "I was telling your daughter Mary about her errors."

"Moll" is a nickname for "Mary."

Yellowhammer said:

"Errors!

"Nay, the city cannot hold you, wife, but you must necessarily fetch words from Westminster."

At the time, "errors" was a legal word that meant "mistakes in law."

Westminister was where justice was administered. Lawyers were well-educated and used fancy words.

Yellowhammer continued:

"I have done, indeed. Has no attorney's clerk been here recently and changed his half-crown piece his mother sent him, or rather cheated you with a gilded twopence, to bring the word in fashion for her faults or cracks in duty and obedience, term them even so, sweet wife?"

He was asking if she, his wife, had been bribed to use such a fancy word.

A twopence is a silver coin; it could be gilded in an attempt to pass it off as a gold coin.

Yellowhammer continued:

"As there is no woman made without a flaw, your purest lawns have frays, and cambrics have bracks."

A flaw can be a crack. No woman is made without a crack in her vulva.

"Bracks" are flaws and faults — and cracks and openings.

"Lawn" and "cambric" are kinds of cloth.

"But it is a husband who solders up all cracks," Maudlin said.

Yes, a husband can fill a vagina.

"Who is he who has come, sir?" Moll asked, changing the subject.

The word "come" can mean "cum."

Yellowhammer said:

"Sir Walter's come. He was met at Holborn Bridge, and in his company is a respectable, fair young gentlewoman, whom I guess by her red hair, and other rank descriptions, is his landed niece brought out of Wales, whom Tim, our son (the Cambridge boy), must marry. It is a match of Sir Walter's own making and arrangement to bind us and our heirs to him forever."

"Rank" can mean 1) abundant, and/or 2) lecherous.

Maudlin said:

"We are honored then, if this baggage would be humble, and kiss him with devotion when he enters."

"This baggage" is Moll, their daughter. Yellowhammer and Maudlin wanted her to marry Sir Walter Whorehound.

One meaning of "baggage" is "a worthless woman."

Maudlin continued:

"I cannot get her for my life to instruct her hand thus, before and after, which a knight will look for, before and after. I have continually told her that it is the waving of a woman that often moves a man and prevails strongly."

A young woman's hands could be positioned before and after (in front and in back) in a fashionable curtsey.

Yes, the waving of a woman before and after — the jiggling of breasts and buttocks — often moves a man (and makes his penis move).

Maudlin continued:

"But sweet, have you sent word to Cambridge? Has Tim received word of this visit?"

Yellowhammer answered, "He had word just the day after when you sent him the silver spoon to eat his broth in the hall, among the gentlemen commoners."

The gentlemen commoners were students at Oxford who paid higher fees and ate at their own table.

"O, it was timely," Maudlin said.

A porter entered the scene.

"How are things now?" Yellowhammer asked.

"A letter from a gentleman in Cambridge has arrived," the porter said.

Yellowhammer said:

"O, one of Hobson's porters, thou are welcome.

"I told thee, Maud, that we should hear from Tim."

Hobson was a very successful carrier. He owned large six- and eight-horse wagons to carry and transport goods.

Yellowhammer read the letter, which was written in Latin, out loud:

"*Amantissimis charissimisque ambobus parentibus patri et matri.*"

["To both my most loving and dearest parents, father and mother."]

"What's the matter?" Maudlin asked.

Tim had written in Latin to his parents, neither of whom knew Latin. A person who has completed the requirements for a bachelor's degree ought to know better than to write in Latin to a person who does not know Latin.

Yellowhammer, who did not know Latin, replied, "Nay, by my truth, I don't know. Don't ask me. He's grown too verbal; this learning is a great witch."

Maudlin, who also did not know Latin, said:

"Please, let me see it. I was accustomed to understand him."

She read out loud:

"*Amantissimus charissimus.*"

She "translated":

"He has sent the carrier's man, he says."

She read out loud:

"*Ambobus parentibus.*"

She "translated":

"For a pair of boots."

The porter was wearing boots.

She read out loud:

"*Patri et matri.*"

She "translated":

"Pay the porter, or it makes no matter."

Maudlin's words meant: Pay the porter, but if you don't, it doesn't matter.

"Matter" means "sense." Maudlin's translation lacked sense to anyone who wanted an accurate translation.

The porter, who also did not know Latin, but who did want to be paid, said:

"Yes, by my faith, mistress, there's no true construction — no accurate translation — in that. I have taken a great deal of pains and have come from the Bell Inn, sweating."

The Bell Inn was a quarter-mile from Yellowhammer's shop.

The porter continued:

"Let me come to it, for I was a scholar forty years ago. The message is thus, I promise you."

He read out loud:

"*Matri.*"

He "translated":

"It makes no matter."

He read out loud:

"*Ambobus parentibus,*"

He "translated":

"For a pair of boots."

He read out loud:

"*Patri.*"

He "translated":

"Pay the porter."

He read out loud:

"*Amantissimis charissimis.*"

He "translated":

"He's the carrier's man, and his name is Sims."

He then said:

"And there he says the truth, indeed. My name is Sims, indeed.

"I have not forgotten all my learning. A money matter, I thought I should hit on it."

He had thought that he would get the part about money right.

"Go, thou are an old fox," Yellowhammer said. "There's a tester for thee."

He tipped the porter with a tester: a coin.

"If I see your worship at Goose Fair, I have a dish of birds for you," the porter said.

Young geese were roasted and sold at the fair at Stratford-le-Bow, which was northeast of London.

"Why, do thou dwell at Bow?" Yellowhammer asked.

"All my lifetime, sir," the porter said. I could always say 'Bo' to a goose. Farewell to your worship."

A person who will not say "Boo" to a goose is timid; therefore, the porter, who will say "Boo" to a goose, is not timid.

"Goose" is Elizabethan and Jacobean slang for "fool."

The porter was calling Yellowhammer, who had called him an old fox, a goose.

He was also saying "Bo," aka "Bow," in answer to Yellowhammer's question.

The porter exited.

"A merry porter," Yellowhammer said.

"How can he choose but to be merry, coming with Cambridge letters from our son, Tim?" Maudlin said.

Returning his attention to the letter, Yellowhammer asked:

"What's here?"

He read out loud:

"*Maximus diligo*."

["The greatest, I love."]

Possibly, Tim's Latin is not good.

Yellowhammer said:

"Indeed, I must go to my learned counsel with this letter. It will never be understood, if I don't."

"Go to my cousin then, at the Inns of Court," Maudlin said.

The Inns of Court were populated by law students.

In Elizabethan and Jacobean times, the word "cousin" meant "kinsman." It had a wider meaning than it does now.

"Bah, they are all for French," Yellowhammer said. "They speak no Latin."

They knew what was called "Law French."

"Law French" is a mongrel form of Latin.

"Then the parson will translate it," Maudlin said.

Yellowhammer said:

"Nay, he disclaims it. He calls Latin Papistry, and he will not deal with it."

The parson was anti-Catholic.

Puritans were anti-Catholic.

A gentleman with a gold chain entered the scene.

A "chain" is a necklace.

Yellowhammer then said:

"What is it you lack, gentleman?"

Tradesmen would say to customers, "What is it you lack?" This meant, "What do you need?"

"Please, weigh this chain," the gentleman said.

Yellowhammer, Maudlin, and Moll paid attention to the gentleman.

Sir Walter Whorehound, a Welsh gentlewoman, and Davy Dahumma entered the scene. Davy was Sir Walter Whorehound's man-servant.

"Now, wench, thou are welcome to the heart of the city of London," Sir Walter Whorehound said.

"*Dugat a whee*," the Welsh gentlewoman said.

["May God preserve you."]

"You can thank me in English if you wish," Sir Walter Whorehound said.

"I can, sir, simply," the Welsh gentlewoman said.

Sir Walter Whorehound said:

"It will serve to pass, wench. It will do. It would be strange if I would lie with thee so often, and then leave thee without English: That would be unnatural.

"I bring thee up to London to turn thee into gold, wench, and make thy fortune shine like a bright trade. A goldsmith's shop sets out a city maiden. It is a suitable setting for a city maiden — it displays her advantageously."

A bright trade may be the profitable trade of goldsmith, or the profitable trade of prostitute.

Prostitutes displayed themselves in bay windows.

Sir Walter Whorehound then said:

"Davy Dahumma, don't say a word."

"Mum, mum, sir," Davy said.

He would remain mum: silent.

"Here you must pass for a pure virgin," Sir Walter Whorehound said to the Welsh gentlewoman.

Davy said to himself, "Pure Welsh virgin! She lost her maidenhead in Brecknockshire."

Brecknockshire is a Welsh county.

"Nock" is Elizabethan and Jacobean slang for "vagina."

"Break nock" is a broken maidenhead.

"I hear you mumble, Davy," Sir Walter Whorehound said.

One meaning of "mumble" is "talk indistinctly."

"I have teeth, sir," Davy said. "I need not mumble yet for the next forty years."

Another meaning of "mumble" is "chew with toothless gums."

"The knave bites plaguily," Sir Walter Whorehound said.

"What's your price, sir?" Yellowhammer said to the gentleman who was hocking the chain.

"A hundred pounds, sir," the gentleman said.

Yellowhammer said:

"A hundred marks at the very most. It is not for me, otherwise."

A mark is two-thirds of a pound.

The gentleman exited with the gold chain.

Seeing the new arrivals, Yellowhammer said:

"What! Sir Walter Whorehound?"

"O death!" Moll said.

Not liking what she saw, she exited.

Maudlin said:

"Why, daughter! Indeed! The baggage!"

Yellowhammer went after Moll.

Maudlin then said to Sir Walter Whorehound:

"She is a bashful girl, sir; these young things are modest. Besides, you have a presence, sweet Sir Walter, that is able to daunt a maiden who is brought up in the city. A brave court spirit makes our virgins quiver and makes them kiss with trembling thighs."

"Trembling knees" or "knee-trembler" refers to sex in a standing position.

Yellowhammer brought Moll back.

Maudlin continued:

"Yet see. Here she comes, sir."

"Why, how are you now, pretty mistress, now I have caught you?" Sir Walter asked. "What! Can you so injure your time that you stray thus from your faithful servant?"

Sir Walter Whorehound was using chivalric language: He was Moll's "servant," aka "male admirer."

Yellowhammer said:

"Bah, stop your words, good knight. It will make her blush if you don't. Those words sound too high and have gone too far for the daughters of the Freedom."

"Daughters of the Freedom" are women who reside in the city of London but not in the court. The Freedom are citizens who have a license to ply their trade, or who have freeman status in a guild. These tradesmen have the freedom to ply their trade in the city of London.

Yellowhammer continued:

"The words 'honor' and 'faithful servant' are compliments for the worthies of Whitehall, or Greenwich. Just plain, sufficient, subsidy words serve us, sir."

Whitehall and Greenwich were the sites of royal palaces.

"Subsidy words" are terms used by businesspeople rather than terms used by courtiers. Successful businesspeople paid a kind of tax known as a subsidy.

Yellowhammer then asked about the Welsh gentlewoman:

"And is this gentlewoman your worthy niece?"

"You may be bold with her on these terms," Sir Walter Whorehound said. "It is she, sir. She is heir to some nineteen mountains."

"Bless us all, you overwhelm me, sir, with love and riches," Yellowhammer said.

"And the mountains are all as high as St. Paul's Cathedral," Sir Walter Whorehound said.

"Here's work, indeed," Davy said.

Sir Walter was working to impress on Yellowhammer that the Welsh gentlewoman would be a good mate for his son, Tim.

"What do thou say, Davy?" Sir Walter Whorehound said.

"Higher, sir, by far," Davy said. "You cannot see the top of the mountains."

Yellowhammer said:

"What, man!

"Maudlin, salute — greet — this gentlewoman, who will be our daughter-in-law if things go well."

Possibly, the Welsh gentlewoman could be married in the future to Tim, the son of Yellowhammer and Maudlin, none of whom knew that the Welsh gentlewoman slept with Sir Walter Whoreson.

Touchwood Junior entered the scene. His older brother, Touchwood Senior, had reduced financial assets.

He said to himself:

"My knight with a brace — a pair — of footmen has come and brought up his ewe mutton — his whore — to find a ram — a husband — at London."

"My knight" is Sir Walter. He was Touchwood Junior's rival for Moll.

Touchwood Junior continued:

"I must hasten it — my marriage to Moll — and I must act quickly, or else I must pick a famine and choose to starve.

"Her blood's mine, and that's the surest.

"Well, knight, that choice spoil is kept only for me."

The "choice spoil" was Moll.

Touchwood Junior wanted to marry Moll. Her "blood" — sexual desire — was for him, as his was for her, and that would be a big help in concluding the marriage.

His rival for Moll's hand in marriage was Sir Walter Whorehound, who was trying to marry off his whore: the Welsh gentlewoman.

Touchwood Junior quietly got Moll's attention from behind her. He did not want to attract others' attention by talking face to face with her.

Moll said quietly to Touchwood Junior, "Sir?"

He handed her a note and said:

"Don't turn to me until thou may lawfully. It just whets my stomach, aka my sexual appetite, which is too sharp set — too eager — already.

"Read that note carefully. Keep me away from suspicion still — don't attract attention to me — nor know my zeal except in thy heart.

"Read and send but thy liking in three words — that is, briefly. I'll be at hand to take it."

"Thy liking" was Moll's consent to marry him.

Yellowhammer, who wanted Sir Walter Whorehound to turn and go inside his — Yellowhammer's house, said:

"O, turn, sir, turn."

He then said about his son, Tim:

"He is a poor plain boy, a university man. He graduates next Lent to a Bachelor of Art. He will get his degree this coming Lent.

"He will be called Sir Yellowhammer then over all Cambridge, and that's half a knight."

A university graduate was called *Dominus*. One translation of *Dominus* is "Sir." For university graduates, "Sir" was used with the surname, aka family name, only. Knights were called "Sir," which was used with their Christian or given name, or with both Christian and family names.

Sir Walter, aka Sir Walter Whorehound, was a knight; if he had not been a knight but had instead been a graduate of Oxford or Cambridge, he would have been called "Sir Whorehound."

"Will it please you to draw near and taste the welcome of the city, sir?" Maudlin asked.

She wanted him to go inside her house.

"Come, good Sir Walter, and your virtuous niece here," Yellowhammer said.

"It is manners to accept kindness," Sir Walter Whorehound said.

"Lead them in, wife," Yellowhammer said to Maudlin.

"Your company, sir," Sir Walter Whorehound said.

"I'll give it to you instantly," Yellowhammer said.

In this society, "instantly" meant "soon."

Sir Walter Whorehound, the Welsh gentlewoman, Davy, and Maudlin exited.

Touchwood Junior said to himself:

"How strangely busy is the devil and riches.

"Moll is a poor soul who is kept in too hard. Her mother's eye is cruel toward her, being turned to him, her husband, supporting him in his effort to arrange a marriage between Moll and Sir Walter.

"It would be a good mirth now to set him — Yellowhammer — to work to make her — Moll's — wedding ring. I must set about it. Rather than the game should fall to a stranger, it would be honesty in me to enrich my father."

If all worked out well, Yellowhammer would become Touchwood Junior's father-in-law, and Touchwood Junior could help enrich him by hiring him to make Moll's wedding ring.

Yellowhammer said to himself about his daughter, Moll:

"The girl is wondrously peevish."

Moll was showing no interest in Sir Walter Whorehound.

Yellowhammer continued talking to himself:

"I fear nothing except that she's taken with some other love; if she is, then all's quite dashed and ended. That must be narrowly and closely looked to. We cannot be too wary when it comes to our children."

Yellowhammer then said to Touchwood Junior, "What is it you lack? What do you need?"

Touchwood Junior said:

"O, nothing now; all that I wish for is present."

Moll was present, and she was all that he wished for.

Touchwood Junior continued:

"I would have a wedding ring made for a gentlewoman, with all speed that may be."

"Of what weight, sir?" Yellowstone said.

"Of some half ounce, which would be set fair and comely with the spark — jewel — of a diamond," Touchwood Junior said. "Sir, it would be a pity to lose the least grace."

Yellowhammer said:

"Please, let's see it."

Touchwood Junior handed him a diamond.

"Indeed, sir, it is a pure one," Yellowhammer said.

"So is the mistress," Touchwood Junior said.

"Have you the wideness of her finger, sir?" Yellowhammer asked.

Touchwood Junior said:

"Yes, surely I think I have her measure about me."

The "measure" can be 1) the size of her finger, or 2) his penis, which could measure a part of her.

He searched his pockets for a paper and then said:

"In good faith, it is down. I cannot show it to you. I must pull too many things out to be certain."

"It is down" can mean 1) the measurement is down too deep in his pocket, and/or 2) his penis is not erect.

Touchwood Junior continued:

"Let me see: long, and slender, and neatly jointed, just such another gentlewoman as is your daughter, sir."

A penis can be long and slender, and it can be neatly jointed — connected — to a vagina.

"And therefore, sir, no gentlewoman," Yellowhammer said.

The Yellowhammer family's social status did not rank so high as gentleman and gentlewoman.

"I say that I never saw two maidens' hands more alike," Touchwood Junior said. "I'll never seek farther, if you'll give me permission, sir."

"If you dare venture by her finger, sir," Yellowhammer said.

Would he accept responsibility if the ring's size turned out to be incorrect? It would be risky to make the ring without first measuring the intended bride's finger.

"Aye, and I'll bide all loss, sir," Touchwood Junior said.

"Say you so, sir," Yellowhammer said. "Let's see you here, girl."

Moll moved closer to them.

"Shall I make bold with your finger, gentlewoman?" Touchwood Junior asked Moll.

"Your pleasure, sir," Moll said.

"That fits her to a hair, sir," Touchwood Junior said. "It fits her exactly."

The finger would exactly fit the ring.

Wedding rings and fingers are symbols of sex.

The hair may be a pubic hair.

"Hair" is a pun on "heir."

"What's your posy now, sir?" Yellowhammer asked.

The posy was a saying that was engraved on the inside of the ring.

"By the Mass, that's true! Posy, indeed," Touchwood Junior said. "Even thus, sir: 'Love that's wise, blinds parents' eyes.'"

"What! What!" Yellowhammer said. "If I may speak without offence, sir, I bet my life —"

"What, sir?" Touchwood Junior asked.

"Come on," Yellowhammer said. "You'll pardon me?"

"Pardon you?" Touchwood Junior said. "Aye, I will, sir."

"Will you, indeed?" Yellowhammer asked.

"Yes, indeed, I will," Touchwood Junior said.

Yellowhammer said:

"You'll steal away some man's daughter. Am I near you? Have I guessed correctly?

"Do you turn aside? You gentlemen are mad wags; I marvel that things can be so warily carried out, and that parents can be so blinded, but they're served right who have two eyes, and wear so dull a sight."

"May thy doom take hold of thee," Touchwood Junior said.

In other words: May what you suspect come true.

"Tomorrow noon shall show your ring well done," Yellowhammer said.

Touchwood Junior said:

"Being so done, it is soon."

In other words: If the work is done well, then that is quick work.

Touchwood Junior continued:

"Thanks, and I take your leave, sweet gentlewoman."

Moll said:

"Sir, you are welcome."

Touchwood Junior exited.

Moll said to herself:

"O, if I were made of wishes, I would have gone with thee."

"Come, now we'll see how the rules — the revels and possibly, agreements — are going inside our house," Yellowhammer said.

"That robs my joy," Moll said. "There I lose all I win."

If she were to marry Sir Walter Whorehound, she would lose all she had won in Touchwood Junior.

They exited.

Using different doors, Davy and Allwit entered a room in Allwit's house. Allwit was married to Mistress Allwit. Davy was Sir Walter Whorehound's man-servant.

"May honesty wash my eyes," Davy said to himself. "I have spied a wittol."

A wittol is a contented cuckold. A cuckold is a man with an unfaithful wife.

Sir Walter Whorehound had been having an affair with Mistress Allwit for many years. She was the mother of his six children, and she was pregnant with his seventh child.

Seeing a wittol made Davy feel as if his eyes had been made dirty.

"What, Davy Dahumma?" Allwit said. "Welcome from North Wales, indeed, and has Sir Walter come?"

"He has newly come to town, sir," Davy said.

"Go inside to the maids, sweet Davy, and give the order to immediately make Sir Walter's chamber ready," Allwit said. "My wife's as great as she can wallow, Davy, and longs for nothing but pickled cucumbers and Sir Walter's coming, and now she shall have it, boy."

Pregnant women sometimes have cravings.

"Pickled" can mean "poxed," a cucumber can be a phallic symbol, and so a pickled cucumber can be a diseased penis.

"Sir Walter's coming" may be "Sir Walter's cumming."

"She's sure to have them, sir," Davy said.

"Thy very sight will hold my wife in pleasure, until the knight comes himself," Allwit said. "Go in, in, in, Davy."

Davy exited further into Allwit's house.

Alone, Allwit said to himself:

"The founder's come to town."

Literally, a founder is a person who endows an institution.

Sir Walter Whorehound was the figurative founder of Allwit's family. He begot the children, and he paid the bills, and Allwit was happy with this arrangement and did not want it to end. Sir Walter had made him prosperous.

If Sir Walter were to marry, then he would start begetting legitimate children, and likely his arrangement with Allwit would end.

Allwit continued saying to himself:

"I am like a man finding a table furnished with provisions at his hand, as mine is still to me. He prays for the founder. Bless the right worshipful, the good founder's life."

Psalm 23:5 states, "*Thou preparest a table before me in the presence of mine enemies; thou anointest my head with oil; my cup runneth over*" (King James Version).

Allwit continued saying to himself:

"I thank him, he has maintained my house for the past ten years. He not only provides for my wife, but he provides for me and for all my family."

The word "family" included the household servants.

Allwit continued saying to himself:

"I am at his table, he begets for me all my children, and he pays the nurse, monthly, or weekly. He puts me to nothing — to no expense. I don't pay rent, nor church dues, not so much as pay for the scavenger: This is the happiest state that a man was ever born to."

A scavenger hired the poor to sweep the streets and keep them clean.

"I walk out in a morning, come to breakfast, find excellent cheer and provisions, have a good fire in winter.

"I look in my coal house about midsummer eve and I see that it is full, with five or six chaldrons, newly laid up."

A chaldron is 36 bushels of coal.

Allwit continued saying to himself:

"If I look in my backyard, I shall find a steeple made up with Kentish faggots, which overlooks the waterhouse and the windmills."

A Kentish faggot is a bundle of brushwood, eight feet long and one foot thick.

Allwit continued saying to himself:

"I say nothing, but I smile and pin — that is, I bolt — the door.

He was a doorkeeper for his wife.

In brothels, a pimp would lock the door and stand outside. When enough time had passed for the whore and customer to have finished, he would let them know.

"When she lies in, awaiting childbirth, as now she's even upon the point of grunting, a lady does not lie in like her."

His wife was almost ready to give birth. She would do so in what comfort money could provide for her.

Allwit continued saying to himself:

"There's her embossings, embroiderings, spanglings, and I don't know what, as if she lay with all the gaudy shops in Gresham's Burse — that is, the Royal Exchange — around her; then there are her restoratives, enough to be able to set up a young apothecary — a young druggist — and richly stock the foreman of a druggist shop.

"Her sugar arrives in whole loaves, and her wines arrive in rundlets."

A sugar-loaf is a cone-shaped quantity of sugar. Sugar snippers were used to cut off pieces of sugar for use in food and drinks.

Rundlets are barrels.

Allwit continued saying to himself:

"I see these things, but like a happy man, I pay for none at all, yet fools think it's mine.

"I have the name — the reputation for being a rich man — and in his gold I shine.

"And where some merchants would in soul kiss hell, to buy a paradise for their wives, and dye their conscience in the bloods of prodigal heirs to deck their night-piece [bed-fellow], yet all this being done, they are eaten with jealousy to the inmost bone — as what affliction more violates the husband's human nature than to feed the wife plump for another's veins — that is, for another's sexual pleasure?"

Some merchants would cheat customers to provide a paradise for their wives, and they would cheat prodigal heirs to buy clothing for their "night-piece," aka bed-companion, who need not always be their own wife. Yet these merchants would feel jealousy; they would worry that they were treating their wives and mistresses well only to be made a cuckold.

In contrast, Allwit was a man who felt no jealousy.

Allwit continued saying to himself:

"These torments stand I freed of. I am as clear from jealousy of a wife as from the charge — from the cost.

"O, two miraculous blessings.

"It is the knight who has taken that labor all out of my hands. I may sit still and play; he's jealous for me — he watches her steps, and he sets spies to watch her.

"I live at ease.

He has both the cost of my living and the torment of what should be my jealousy. When the strings of his heart fret, I feed, laugh, or sing, 'La dildo, dildo la dildo, la dildo dildo de dildo.'"

Some people in this society believed that the heart was supported by strings. When the heartstrings broke, the person died.

A dildo is an artificial penis. It is a substitute for the real thing. Allwit's real thing was unemployed — unless his wife was cheating on Sir Walter with him.

Two servants entered the scene.

"What has he got singing in his head now?" the first servant asked.

"Now that he's out of work, he falls to making dildoes," the second servant said.

The servants believed that Allwit's penis was not being used to have sex with his wife.

"Now, sirs, Sir Walter's come," Allwit said.

"Has our master come?" the first servant asked.

"Your master?" Allwit said. "What am I?"

"Don't you know, sir?" the first servant asked.

"Tell me, aren't I your master?" Allwit asked.

"O, you are only our mistress' husband," the first servant said.

In this context, a mistress is a female boss.

"Ergo, knave, I am your master," Allwit said.

"Ergo" means "therefore."

Allwit had more respect for himself than the servants had for him.

The first servant said:

"*Negatur argumentum.*"

["Your argument is denied."]

The first servant then said:

"Here comes Sir Walter."

Sir Walter Whorehound and Davy entered the scene.

Allwit took off his hat to show respect to Sir Walter. Servants were bare-headed when in the presence of their masters.

The first servant then said:

"Now he stands bare-headed as well as we; make the most of him, he's but one peep above a serving-man, and so much his horns make him."

"One peep" is "one degree."

Allwit was wearing the invisible horns of a cuckold. They metaphorically made him a little taller than a servant.

"How are thou, Jack?" Sir Walter asked Allwit.

"Proud of your worship's health, sir," Allwit said.

"How is your wife?" Sir Walter asked.

"Even after your own making, sir," Allwit said. "She's a tumbler, indeed; the nose and belly meet."

A "tumbler" is a sexually active person. Mistress Allwit's nose and belly were close together because her pregnancy was well-advanced.

"They'll part in time again," Sir Walter said.

"At the good hour, they will, if it pleases your worship," Allwit said.

Sir Walter said:

"Here, sirrah, pull off my boots."

A servant pulled off Sir Walter's boots.

Sir Walter then said:

"Put on, put on, Jack."

Allwit's first name may be "John," for which "Jack" is a nickname. But "Jack" is a word used for a contemptible fellow.

Hats were customarily worn indoors as well as outdoors.

Sir Walter wanted Allwit to put his hat back on.

"I thank your kind worship, sir," Allwit said.

"Slippers!" Sir Walter said. "By God's heart, you are sleepy."

His slippers should have already been brought to him.

A servant brought him slippers.

Allwit said to himself, "The game begins already."

Sir Walter enjoyed asserting his authority.

"Bah, put on your hat, Jack," Sir Walter said.

Allwit said to himself:

"Now I must do it, or he'll be as angry now as if I had put it on at first bidding."

Sir Walter would have been angry if Allwit had put on his hat the first time that Sir Walter told him to.

Allwit continued saying to himself:

"It is but observing: deference paid to a superior. It is but observing a man's humor — his disposition — once, and you may have him by the nose all his life."

Who was having whom by the nose? Was Allwit having Sir Walter by the nose? Was Sir Walter having Allwit by the nose? Both?

Both men seemed to like the arrangement they had made.

"Having someone by the nose" means "having someone at your mercy."

Bulls could be led by the nose when they wore a nose-ring.

Allwit put his hat back on his head.

"What entertainment has lain open here?" Sir Walter asked. "No strangers in my absence?"

Mistress Allwit's legs could be open and provide entertainment.

"To be sure, sir, not any," the first servant said.

Allwit said to himself, "His jealousy begins. Aren't I happy now who can laugh inward while his marrow melts?"

Sir Walter's marrow could melt because of the heat generated by jealousy.

"How do you satisfy me?" Sir Walter asked.

Sir Walter wanted a reason to believe the first servant.

"Good sir, be patient," the first servant said.

"For two months' absence, I'll be satisfied," Sir Walter said.

"No living creature entered —" the first servant said.

"Entered?" Sir Walter asked. "Come, swear —"

He was worried about a penis other than his own entering Mistress Allwit's vagina.

"You will not hear me out and let me finish, sir —" the first servant said.

"Yes, I'll hear it out, sir," Sir Walter said.

"Sir, he can tell himself," the first servant said.

Allwit could answer the question: Has anyone been sleeping with Allwit's wife while Sir Walter was gone?

Sir Walter said:

"By God's heart, he can tell!

"Do you think I'll trust him? I'll trust him as I would a usurer — moneylender — with forfeited lordships."

A forfeited lordship was mortgaged property that had been seized to repay debts.

In other words: I'll trust him not at all.

Sir Walter continued:

"Him? O monstrous injury! Believe him? Can the devil speak ill of darkness?"

He then asked Allwit:

"What can you say, sir?"

Allwit said, "By my soul and conscience, sir, she's a wife as honest of her body to me as any lord's proud lady can be."

Mistress Allwit had not slept with anyone, including Allwit, while Sir Walter was gone. So said Allwit.

"Yet, by your leave, I heard you were once offering to go to bed to her," Sir Walter said.

"No, I protest, sir," Allwit said.

No, he had not attempted to sleep with his own wife. So said Allwit.

Sir Walter said, "By God's heart, if you do, you shall take all — I'll marry."

This was a threat. If Allwit slept with his own wife, he would have to take everything that went with having a wife, including the bills.

To Allwit, this was frightening.

He said, "O, I beseech you, sir —"

"That wakes the slave, and keeps his flesh in awe," Sir Walter said to himself.

In this context, "slave" means "wretch."

Allwit said to himself:

"I'll stop that gap — that rumor — wherever I find it open; I have poisoned his hopes in marriage already — some old rich widows, and some landed virgins —"

Allwit would do what he could to keep Sir Walter Whorehound from marrying.

"Landed virgins" were virgins who had land.

Sir Walter was interested in wealth and in sex.

Two children, Wat and Nick, entered the scene. Their father was Sir Walter, and their mother was Allwit's wife.

Allwit continued saying to himself:

"And I'll fall to work still before I'll lose him. He's yet too sweet to part from."

He wanted Sir Walter to keep paying the bills of his — Allwit's — household.

"God-den, father," Wat said to Allwit.

"God-den" was used any time after noon; it meant "Good evening."

"Ha, villain, peace," Allwit said to himself.

"God-den, father," Nick said to Allwit.

Allwit said to himself:

"Peace, bastard. If he — Sir Walter — should hear them!"

He said out loud:

"These are two foolish children. They do not know the gentleman who sits there."

The two children did not know that Sir Walter was their father.

Sir Walter said, "O Wat, how do thou, Nick? Go to school. Ply your books, boys, huh?"

Wat and Nick exited.

Allwit then said to himself:

"Where's your legs, whoresons? They should kneel indeed if they could say their prayers."

He wanted the children to bow to show respect to Sir Walter.

And if the children knew that Sir Walter was their father, they should kneel before him and ask him for a blessing, as was the custom in this society.

Sir Walter said to himself:

"Let me see, stay, how shall I dispose of these two brats now when I am married, for they must not mingle among my children whom I get in wedlock — that would make foul work and raise many storms.

"I'll bind Wat as an apprentice to a goldsmith, my father Yellowhammer, as fit as can be. Nick I'll bind as an apprentice with some vintner."

"My father Yellowhammer" is "my future father-in-law Yellowhammer."

"Good, goldsmith and vintner; there will be wine in bowls, indeed."

Wat would provide the bowls, and Nick would provide the wine.

Allwit's heavily pregnant wife, Mistress Allwit, entered the scene.

She said to Sir Walter, "Sweet knight, welcome. I have all my longings now in town. Now well-come the good hour."

"How cheers my mistress?" Sir Walter asked.

"Made lightsome, even by him who made me heavy," Mistress Allwit said.

Sir Walter had made her pregnant. Now his presence made her happy.

"I think she shows gallantly, like a moon at full, sir," Sir Walter said to Allwit.

"True, and if she bears a male child, there's the man in the moon, sir," Allwit said.

"It is but the boy in the moon yet, goodman calf," Sir Walter said.

A "calf" is a fool.

"There was a man," Allwit said. "The boy had never been there else."

The man had made a woman pregnant with a boy.

"It shall be yours, sir," Sir Walter said.

Mistress Allwit and Sir Walter exited together.

Alone, Allwit said to himself, "No, by my truth, I'll swear it's none of mine; let him who begot it keep it. Thus do I rid myself of fear, lie soft, sleep hard, drink wine, and eat good cheer — good food."

He exited.

CHAPTER 2

— 2.1 —

Touchwood Senior and his wife talked together on a street. Their finances were in poor shape, and they were going to live apart from each other in order to save on expenses.

Mistress Touchwood said, "It will be so tedious, sir, to live apart from you, but that necessity must be obeyed."

Touchwood Senior said:

"I wish that it might not be necessary to live apart from each other, wife. The tediousness will be for the most part mine because I understand the blessings — the happiness and the children — I have in thee. To part in this way drives the torment to a knowing and understanding heart.

"But as thou say, we must give way to need and necessity and live awhile asunder from each other. Our desires are both too fruitful for our barren fortunes.

"How adverse runs the destiny of some creatures — some can only get riches and no children, but we can get only children and no riches.

"So then it is the most prudent part to check our wills and sexual desires, and until our fortunes rise, make our bloods — our sexual passions — lie still."

Touchwood Senior then said to himself:

"By God's life, every year a child, and some years two, besides drinkings outside the house, which are never reckoned. This gear will not hold out."

Their expenses were high. For one thing, every year Mistress Touchwood gave birth to one or two children. Also, as will become clear, Touchwood Senior had many affairs and many bastards. His "drinkings outside the house" are probably a veiled reference to these affairs. These affairs generated many bastards — so many bastards that he did not know their exact number.

This society existed before effective birth control was widely available.

"Gear" can mean 1) situation, and 2) sex organs.

So far, Touchwood Senior's penis was holding out just fine.

"Sir, for a time, I'll take the courtesy — the hospitality — of my uncle's house, if you are pleased to like it and agree," Mistress Touchwood said, "until prosperity look with a friendly eye upon our states and fortunes."

Touchwood Senior said:

"Honest wife, I thank thee. I never knew the perfect treasure thou brought with thee more than at this exact minute. When he's at his poorest, a man's happy who has matched his soul as rightly as his body.

"Had I married a sensual fool now, as it is hard to escape doing so among gentlewomen of our time, she would have hanged about my neck, and never left her hold until she had kissed me into wanton businesses, which at the waking of my better judgment, I would have cursed most bitterly, and laid a thicker vengeance on my act than misery of the birth, which would be enough if it were born to greatness, whereas my offspring is sure to have beggary, even though it were begotten in wine.

"Fulness of joy shows the goodness in thee. Thou are a matchless wife. Farewell, my joy."

"Matchless" means 1) incomparable, and 2) without a husband.

"I shall not lack seeing you?" Mistress Touchwood asked.

Touchwood Senior said, "I'll see thee often, talk in mirth, and play at kisses with thee, anything, wench, but what may beget beggars. There I give over the set, throw down the cards, and dare not take them up."

He promised to see her, but to avoid having sex with her, lest the sex result in another mouth to feed. Sex was a game that he would not play with her.

"Your will is mine, sir," Mistress Touchwood said.

She exited.

Alone, Touchwood Senior said to himself:

"This not only makes her honesty and chasteness perfect, but also her discretion, and this proves and confirms her good judgment.

"Had her desires been wanton, they'd been blameless in being lawful always because we are married, but of all creatures I hold that wife a most unmatched treasure who can fix her pleasure to her fortunes, and not to her blood, aka her passion — this is like wedlock."

His wife was willing to live apart from him and not have sex with him because their finances would not allow it.

Touchwood Senior continued:

"The feast of marriage is not lust but love, and care of the estate. When I please blood, I merrily sing, and suck out others' blood."

"Sing" can metaphorically mean "have sex."

"Blood" can mean "sexual passion."

When Touchwood Senior has sex and pleases his sexual passion, he sucks out — draws forth — the sexual passion of his partner. Both he and his sex partner enjoy themselves.

But the sentence is ambiguous. "Suck out others' blood" may be negative. In that case, Touchwood Senior enjoys the sex, but his partner, in the case of extramarital affairs, may not. Or, if she enjoys the sex, she nevertheless suffers a negative result: giving birth to a bastard. In such a case, Touchwood Senior not only sings, but also stings.

Touchwood Senior continued:

"In such a case, it is many a wise man's fault, but of all men I am the most unfortunate in that game that has always pleased both genders.

"I never played yet under a bastard."

This means that his affairs always result in a bastard.

A bastard card is a single card left in the hand of a card player. Card players do not want bastard cards.

Touchwood Senior continued:

"The poor wenches curse me to the pit of Hell wherever I come; they were never served so but used to have more words than one to a bargain."

The women he slept with did not expect to become pregnant after just one act of copulation, but Touchwood Senior's sperm cells were vigorous.

Also, the women he slept with were accustomed to have more conversation with their lovers than they had with Touchwood Senior. As a much-experienced adulterer, he was a fast worker. Possibly, they expected to have more say in whether they slept with him.

Touchwood Senior continued:

"I have such a fatal finger in such business that I must go forth with it, chiefly for country wenches, for every harvest I shall hinder hay-making."

This "finger" was below his belly button.

His making country wenches pregnant or keeping them busy with sex reduced the workforce when it was time to harvest hay.

Touchwood Senior continued:

"I had no less than seven lie in, awaiting childbirth, the last Progress, within three weeks of one another's time."

A Progress is a visit of the king to various parts of the country. Usually, this happened in high summer: July and August.

A wench carrying a child entered the scene.

"O Snap-hance, have I found you?" she asked.

A snap-hance is a flint-lock on a musket. The flint-lock ignites touchwood in the musket's touchhole. Figuratively, the image is of a penis ejaculating in a vagina.

"Why do you call me Snap-hance?" Touchwood Senior asked.

Displaying the child, the wench said:

"Do you see your workmanship?

"Nay, don't turn away from it, nor attempt to escape, for if you do, I'll cry — proclaim — it through the streets, and follow you.

"Your name may well be called Touchwood, a pox on you, You do but touch and take."

"Touch and take" referred to touching fire to a musket's touchhole and firing. Touchwood Senior did a lot of touching and ejaculating, resulting in impregnation.

Touchwood is tinder; it takes — is set on — fire easily.

"Touch" refers to sexual touching, especially without consent. Touchwood Senior touches women — perhaps with or without consent — and he takes what he wants.

The wench continued:

"Thou have undone — have ruined — me."

Angry, the wench was beginning to use the less respectful "thou" when talking to Touchwood Senior, rather than the respectful "you."

The wench continued:

"I was a maiden — a virgin — before; I can bring a certificate for it from both the churchwardens."

Churchwardens sometimes gave character witnesses. Not all churchwardens were reputable.

"I'll have the parson's hand — that is, his signature — too, or I'll not yield to it," Touchwood Senior replied.

The parson had more moral authority than the churchwardens.

The wench said, "Thou shall have more, thou villain; nothing grieves me except that thou have quite cracked — broken — the marriage of Ellen, my poor cousin in Derbyshire. She'll have a bout with thee.

As used by the woman, the word "bout" meant "lawsuit."

"Indeed, when she will, I'll have a bout with her." Touchwood Senior said.

He meant a bout of sex.

"A law bout, sir, I mean," the wench said.

Touchwood Senior said:

"True, lawyers use such bouts as other men do, and if that is all thy grief, I'll tender — provide for — her a husband. I keep for that purpose two or three gulls in pickle to eat such mutton with, and she shall choose one."

"Gulls" are fools. "In pickle" means "kept in reserve until needed, like foods pickled to preserve them."

A pickling tub was a sweating vat used to treat venereal disease.

Seagulls can be eaten.

"Mutton" is slang for "whore."

Touchwood Senior continued:

"Do but in courtesy, in faith, wench, excuse me of this half yard of flesh, in which I think it wants — lacks — a nail or two."

The half yard of flesh was the child.

A "nail" is one-sixteenth of a yard.

The children of syphilitics sometimes were born without fingernails. They were also often smaller than other children.

The wench said about the child, "No, thou shall find, villain, it has the right shape, and all the nails it should have."

"Indeed, I am poor," Touchwood Senior said. "Do a charitable deed, wench. I am a younger brother, and I have nothing."

This society followed the practice of primogeniture: The eldest son inherited the bulk — or all — of the father's wealth.

Touchwood Senior either had an older brother, or he was lying about having an older brother.

He did have a younger brother: Touchwood Junior.

"Nothing!" the wench said. "Thou have too much, thou lying villain, unless thou were more thankful."

"Nothing" can be "no thing." Touchwood Senior definitely had a thing between his legs.

Touchwood Senior had a lot of sex — too much, if he had sex without consent and without being thankful for the sex the way that loving couples can be.

Touchwood Senior said:

"I have no dwelling; I broke up house just this morning.

"Please pity me, I am a good fellow; indeed, I have been too kind to people of your gender. If I have it without — outside — my belly, none of your sex shall want — lack — it."

A "good fellow" is 1) a good man, or 2) a partier.

"If I have it outside my belly" may mean "if I have anything" or he may be referring to his penis.

According to his words, Touchwood Senior was willing to share with a woman what he had outside.

Men have an outie. Women have an innie. The two fit together.

Touchwood Senior said to himself, "That word — 'it,' aka penis — has been of force, aka efficacious, to move — persuade — a woman."

He then said to the wench:

"There are tricks enough to rid thy hand of the child, wench. Leave it on some rich man's porch, tomorrow before daybreak, or else sooner during this evening. There are twenty devices — ways — to rid thy hand of the child."

He offered her his purse — container for money — and added:

"Here's all I have, indeed; take purse and all."

He then said to himself:

"And I wish I were rid of all the ware in the shop so."

He would like to be rid of all his other bastards — and his wenches — when he was done with them.

"Where I find manly dealings, I am pitiful: full of pity," the wench said. "This shall not trouble you."

"And I say, wench, the next child I'll keep myself," Touchwood Senior said. The wench said:

"Wait, let it be begotten first."

She then said to herself:

"This is the fifth; if ever I venture more where I now walk as if I were a maiden, may I ride for a whore."

The fifth may be 1) her fifth lover, or 2) her fifth child.

Possibly, the wench was promiscuous, got pregnant, and then extorted money from all the possible fathers.

Prostitutes were punished by being put on a cart and paraded through the streets. Often, they were whipped.

"Ride" can also refer to "sexual riding."

The wench exited with the child.

Alone, Touchwood Senior said to himself:

"What shift — arrangement — she'll make now with this piece of flesh — with this baby — in this strict time of Lent, I cannot imagine."

Lent is a time of fasting from flesh.

Touchwood Senior continued saying to himself:

"Flesh dares not peep abroad now.

"I have known this city of London now more than these past seven years, but I protest that I never knew it yet in better — stricter — state of government, nor ever heard of it."

The London he knew no longer existed.

Touchwood Senior continued saying to himself:

"There have been more religious wholesome laws in the half circle of a year — six months — erected for common good, than memory ever knew of, except for the corruption of promoters, and other poisonous officers who infect and with a venomous breath taint every goodness."

"Promoters" are informers. They would inform on people who violated Lenten rules.

Sir Oliver Kix and his wife, Lady Kix, entered the scene.

"O, that I was ever begotten, or bred, or born," Lady Kix complained.

"Be content, sweet wife," Sir Oliver Kix said.

Touchwood Senior said:

"What's here to do now? I bet my life she's in deep passion — starved — because of the imprisonment of veal and mutton now kept in garrets."

During Lent, people were forbidden to eat veal and mutton. Some people attempted to avoid the restriction by keeping veal and mutton in attic garrets.

Yes, Lady Kix lacked "meat," but as the audience soon will learn, she lacked the "meat" that would get her pregnant.

Touchwood Senior added:

"She weeps for some calf's head now; I think her husband's head might serve with bacon."

"Calf" is Elizabethan and Jacobean slang for "fool."

Touchwood Junior entered the scene. He was Touchwood Senior's younger brother.

"Hist," Lady Kix said. "Be quiet."

"Patience, sweet wife," Sir Oliver Kix said.

"Brother, I have been searching for you very hard," Touchwood Junior said.

"Why, what's the business?" Touchwood Senior asked.

"With all speed thou can, procure a marriage license for me," Touchwood Junior said.

"What!" Touchwood Senior said. "A marriage license?"

"By God's foot, she's lost to me if you don't get it," Touchwood Junior said. "I shall miss her forever."

"Nay, to be sure thou shall not miss so fair a mark for thirteen shillings fourpence," Touchwood Senior said.

A mark is a target, and thirteen shillings fourpence was the cost of a marriage license.

"I give you thanks by the hundreds," Touchwood Junior said.

Touchwood Junior and Touchwood Senior exited.

Touchwood Senior quickly returned and eavesdropped, unseen by the Kixes.

Sir Oliver Kix said to his wife, "Nay, please cease, I'll be at more cost yet to find a cure. Thou know we are rich enough."

Lady Kix said:

"All but in blessings, and there the beggar goes beyond us."

Sir Oliver Kix and Lady Kix could not have children, but beggars could.

Lady Kix continued:

"O, O, O, to be seven years a wife and not have a child! O, not have a child!"

An "O" can be a vagina.

"Sweet wife, have patience," Sir Oliver said.

"Can any woman have a greater cut?" Lady Kix said.

A "cut" can be 1) a misfortune, or 2) a vulva.

A cut can also be a gelding: a castrated male.

Sir Oliver said:

"I know it is great, but what of that, wife?"

"It is great" can mean 1) your misfortune is great, or 2) your vagina is large.

Sir Oliver Kix continued:

"I cannot do withal."

This meant: 1) I cannot have children and 2) I cannot have sex with it (your cut, or vagina).

Sir Oliver Kix continued:

"There are things making by thine own doctor's advice at the apothecary's."

He was hoping that the pharmacist might have a cure for his — Sir Oliver's — impotence.

Sir Oliver Kix continued:

"I spare for nothing, wife, no; if the price were forty marks a spoonful, I'd give a thousand pounds to purchase fruitfulness."

He spared nothing for "no thing," That is, he spared no money in an attempt to get his "no thing" — his impotent penis — to work as it ought to work.

Touchwood Senior had been eavesdropping. Now he smiled and exited.

Sir Oliver Kix continued:

"It is but bating — diminishing — so many good works in the erecting of Bridewells and spital-houses, and so fetch it up again, for having no biological children, I intend to make good deeds my metaphorical children."

He could not erect his penis, or not often erect his penis, but he could erect houses of correction for prostitutes, and he could erect hospitals that treated venereal disease.

To get a cure for impotence, he was willing to use some of the money he used for good deeds.

"Give me but those good deeds, and I'll find children," Lady Kix said.

To her, "good deeds" were acts that resulted in children, but she preferred biological children to metaphorical children. That was the kind of erection she was interested in.

"Hang thee, thou have had too many," Sir Oliver said.

Possibly, sometimes he could get and use an erection, but his sperm cells were not as vigorous as the sperm cells of someone such as Touchwood Senior.

Of course, it could be (or could also be) the case that Lady Kix was barren.

"Thou lie, brevity," Lady Kix said.

"Brevity" referred to his sexual shortcomings.

"O horrible, dare thou call me brevity?" Sir Oliver Kix said. "Dare thou be so short with — so rude to — me?"

"Thou deserve worse," Lady Kix said. "Just think about the splendid lands and livings that are kept back through want of it."

They needed children who would inherit their property.

"Don't talk about it, please, or thou shall make me play the woman — that is, act like a woman — and weep, too," Sir Oliver Kix said.

Lady Kix said, "It is our dry barrenness that puffs up Sir Walter — no one gets anything by your not-getting, except that knight. He's made by the means, and he fattens his fortune shortly in a great dowry with a goldsmith's daughter."

Sir Walter Whorehound would inherit the Kixes' lands and wealth if Sir Oliver and Lady Kix did not produce an heir. He was using his anticipated future wealth to court the goldsmith's daughter: Moll.

"They may all be deceived," Sir Oliver Kix said. "Just be patient, wife."

He was still hopeful of producing an heir.

"I have suffered a long time," Lady Kix said.

"Suffer thy heart out," Sir Oliver Kix said. "May a pox torment thee!"

"Nay, may it torment thee, thou desertless slave!" Lady Kix said.

Sir Oliver Kix said:

"Come, come, I have finished.

"You'll go to the gossiping — the christening — of Mr. Allwit's child?"

Lady Kix said:

"Yes, to my much joy."

She was sarcastic.

Lady Kix continued:

"Everyone begets before me — there's my sister who was married just at the most recent Bartholomew Eve, and she can have two children at a birth. O, one of them, one of them would have served my turn."

Bartholomew Eve is August 23. The current time is not yet mid-Lent Sunday, which is the fourth Sunday during Lent. Lent is the 40 days from Ash

Wednesday to Holy Thursday, which is just before Good Friday. In 1613, the date of Ash Wednesday was March 17.

Lady Kix' sister's children were either born prematurely or were conceived before their parents married.

"May sorrow consume thee," Sir Oliver Kix said. "Thou are still crossing me, and thou know my nature."

A maid, whose name was Jugg, entered the scene.

She said to herself:

"O mistress, weeping or railing. That's our house harmony."

Lady Kix did a lot of complaining and a lot of crying.

"What do thou have to say, Jugg?" Lady Kix asked.

"The sweetest news," Jugg the maid said.

"Jugg" is a nickname for a woman named "Joan."

"What is it, wench?" Lady Kix asked.

"Throw down your doctor's drugs," Jugg the maid said. "They're all just heretics. I bring a certain remedy that has been taught, and has been proven, and has never failed."

Some doctors were accused of practicing magic.

"O that! That! That or nothing," Sir Oliver said.

"There's a gentleman," Jugg the maid said. "I happily happen to have his name, too. He has begotten nine children by one water that he uses. It never misses; they come so fast upon him that he was fain — eager — to give it over — to give up sex."

"Water" can be a medicinal drink.

But "water" is also Elizabethan and Jacobean slang for "semen."

"What is his name, sweet Jugg?" Lady Kix asked.

Jugg the maid answered, "One Mr. Touchwood, a fine gentleman, but run behindhand much with begetting children."

Touchwood Senior was impoverished because of his many children.

"Run behindhand much" means that he was much in debt.

"Is it possible?" Sir Oliver Kix asked.

"Why, sir, he'll undertake using that water, within fifteen years, for all your wealth, to make you a poor man because you shall so swarm with children," Jugg the maid said.

Hmm.

It sounds as if Touchstone Senior wanted Sir Oliver to pay him to have sex with Lady Kix.

"I'll venture that, indeed," Sir Oliver Kix said.

"That you shall, husband," Lady Kix said.

"But I must tell you first, he's very dear — very expensive," Jugg the maid said.

"That doesn't matter," Sir Oliver Kix said. "What is wealth for?"

Lady Kix said, "True, sweet husband."

Sir Oliver Kix said, "There's land to come in inheritance if we produce an heir. Put case — that is, suppose — his water stands me in — that is, costs me — some five hundred pounds a pint. It will fetch a thousand pounds, and a Kersten — a Christian — soul."

The word "case" can mean "vagina." The word "water" can mean "semen." The word "stand" can mean "erection."

Lady Kix said, "And that's worth all, sweet husband."

"I'll go about it," Sir Oliver Kix said.

They exited.

Alone on a street, Allwit said to himself:

"I'll go summon gossips — witnesses and godparents — to attend the christening immediately myself; that's all the work I'll do, nor do I need to stir, except that it is my pleasure to walk forth and air myself a little. I am tied to nothing in this business — what I do is merely recreation, not constraint.

"Here's running to and fro, nurse upon nurse, three charwomen, besides maids and neighbors' children. Bah, what a trouble I have rid my hands of. It makes me sweat to think of it."

Sir Walter Whorehound entered the scene.

"How are things now, Jack?" he asked.

Allwit replied:

"I am going to summon gossips for your worship's child, sir."

The gossips were female friends and godparents, who could be male or female.

Allwit continued:

"She is a splendid girl; indeed, I give you joy on her — I congratulate you. She looks as if she had two thousand pounds for her portion — her marriage dowry — and ran away with a tailor because her clothing is so fine. She is a fine, plump, black-eyed slut, under correction, sir. I take delight in seeing her."

A slut is a slovenly female. Infants can be messy.

"Under correction" means "if you don't mind my saying so."

Allwit then called:

"Nurse!"

A dry nurse entered the scene. A dry nurse takes care of children, but she does not breastfeed them.

"Do you call, sir?" the dry nurse asked.

"I am not calling you," Allwit said. "I am calling the wet nurse here. Give me the wet nurse."

A wet nurse does breastfeed the babies of other women.

The dry nurse exited, and a wet nurse, who was carrying a baby girl, entered the scene.

Allwit said:

"Aye, it is thou. Come here, come here.

"Let's see her once again; I cannot choose but to buss her — kiss her — three times in each hour."

The wet nurse said, "You may be proud of it, sir. It is the best piece of work that you ever did."

"Do thou think so, Nurse?" Allwit asked. "What do thou say about Wat and Nick?"

Sir Walter Whorehound was the father of Wat, Nick, and the new infant.

The wet nurse said, "They're pretty children both, but here's a wench who will be a knocker."

A knocker is 1) a knockout — a good-looking person, and/or 2) good in bed.

Allwit said to the infant:

"Pup."

"Pup" is a term of affection.

He then said to the wet nurse:

"Do thou say so to me?"

He then said to the baby girl:

"Pup, little countess."

The baby girl did not actually have the title of "countess." Allwit was punning on "cunt."

Allwit then said to Sir Walter:

"In faith, sir, I thank your worship for this girl ten thousand times, and upward."

"I am glad I have had her for you, sir," Sir Walter Whorehound said to Allwit.

"Here, take her in, Nurse," Allwit said to the wet nurse. "Wipe her and give her spoonmeat."

Spoonmeat is soft food.

The wet nurse said to herself, "Wipe your mouth, sir."

Proverbs 30:20 states, "*This is the way of an adulterous woman: She eats and wipes her mouth, and says, 'I have done no wickedness'*" (King James Version).

But the wet nurse was probably calling Allwit a fool for suggesting that she wean a new infant.

Although Allwit's wife had had seven children, he did not know much about children.

The wet nurse exited.

"And now to see about these gossips," Allwit said.

"Get only two gossips," Sir Walter Whorehound said. "I'll stand for one myself."

"You will be godparent to your own child, sir?" Allwit asked.

"It is the better policy, for it prevents suspicion that I am the father," Sir Walter Whorehound said. "It is good to play with — that is, forestall — rumor at all weapons — that is, with any means available."

"Truly, I commend your care, sir," Allwit said. "It is a thing that I should never have thought of."

Sir Walter Whorehound said to himself:

"He is all the more slave.

"When a man turns base, out goes his soul's pure, holy flame.

"The fat of ease overthrows the eyes of shame."

"I have been studying and thinking about who to get as a godmother who would be suitable to your worship," Allwit said. "Now I have thought of it."

Sir Walter Whorehound said:

"I'll relieve you of that care, and please myself in it."

He then said to himself:

"My love, the goldsmith's daughter, will be godmother. If I send for her, her father will command her to come."

He then called:

"Davy Dahumma!"

Davy entered the scene.

Allwit said, "I'll fit and match your worship then with a male partner."

The male partner would be a male godparent.

Usually, there are two godparents: one male and one female. The number of godparents, however, can vary.

"Who is he?" Sir Walter Whorehound asked.

"A kind, proper gentleman, brother to Mr. Touchwood," Allwit answered.

By "Mr. Touchwood," he meant Touchwood Senior.

"I know Touchwood," Sir Walter Whorehound said. "Has he a brother living?"

Allwit said, "He is a neat — an elegant — bachelor."

Touchwood Junior was a bachelor.

Sir Walter Whorehound said:

"Now we know him, we'll make shift — we'll be content — with him. Dispatch, hurry, the time draws near. Get busy.

"Come here, Davy."

Sir Walter Whorehound and Davy exited.

Alone, Allwit said to himself:

"In truth, I pity him; he never stands still.

"Poor knight, what pains he takes — he sends this way one person, that way he sends another person, so that he hasn't an hour's leisure —

"I would not have thy toil, for all thy pleasure."

Two promoters entered the scene. Promoters looked for people who violated the regulations regarding behavior during Lent. If they found someone eating meat during Lent, they would inform on that person. Unscrupulous promoters could be bribed to not inform on Lenten violators.

Allwit continued saying to himself:

"Ha! What is this now? Who are these men who stand so close at the street corner, pricking up their ears, and snuffing up their noses, like rich men's dogs when the first course of a meal goes in? By the mass, they are promoters. It is so, I bet my life, and they are planted there to arrest the dead corpses of poor calves and sheep, like ravenous creditors who will not allow the bodies of their poor departed debtors to go to the grave, but even in death will vex and stay — halt and delay — the corpses with bills of Middlesex."

"Bills of Middlesex" authorized the arrest of people in Middlesex on false charges. After a person was arrested, real charges were issued. This was a way to get around restrictions on jurisdiction.

Allwit continued saying to himself:

"This Lent will fatten the whoresons up with sweetbreads and lard their whores with lamb-stones."

Sweetbreads — an animal's pancreas, or its thymus gland — were thought to be aphrodisiacs.

Lamb-stones are lamb testicles; they were believed to be aphrodisiacs.

Allwit was well aware that many promoters were corrupt.

Among other things, the promoters would seize meat and then they and their wives and girlfriends would eat it.

Allwit continued:

"What their golls — their hands — can clutch goes presently to their Molls and Dolls."

"Moll" and "Doll" were names used for whores and the girlfriends of criminals.

Allwit continued saying to himself:

"The bawds will be so fat with what they earn that their chins will hang like udders by Easter Eve, and being stroked, will give the milk of witches."

Easter Eve is the end of Lent.

A stereotype of bawds was that they were double-chinned.

Some people in this society believed that witches gave suck with a third nipple to the Devil or to their familiar spirits.

Allwit continued saying to himself:

"How did the mongrels hear that my wife lies in?"

A woman lying in — lying in childbed — would need nourishment.

Promoters knew that, and they could try to catch the husband taking meat to his wife.

Allwit continued saying to himself:

"Well, I may baffle them gallantly."

He could bait — torment — the informers.

Allwit said out loud:

"Pardon me, gentlemen, I am a stranger both to the city and to her carnal strictness."

"Good man," the first promoter said. "What do you want, sir?"

"Please tell me where one dwells who kills this Lent," Allwit requested.

He was saying that he was looking for a butcher.

Butchering animals and eating meat were forbidden during Lent, and informers looked for people who violated Lenten regulations; they made money by turning in such violators of the regulations, or by being bribed not to turn them in.

"What!" the first promoter said. "Kills?"

He whispered to the second promoter, "Come here, Dick, a bird, a bird."

A bird is a victim.

"What is it that you would have?" the second promoter asked Allwit.

"Indeed, any flesh, but I long especially for veal and green sauce," Allwit said.

"Veal" and "green" were associated with gullibility.

"To eat veal and green sauce" meant "to be cheated."

Green sauce could be used to disguise badly cooked meat.

The first promoter said to himself, "Green goose, you shall be sauced."

A green goose is 1) a young goose, or 2) a cuckold.

"I have half a scornful stomach," Allwit said. "No fish will be admitted."

He was saying that he was partially observing Lent. He would eat meat, but he would not eat fish.

Usually, fish can be eaten during Lent, but Orthodox Christians regarded any creature with a backbone, including fish, as meat.

"Not this Lent, sir?" the first promoter asked.

"Lent, what cares colon here for Lent?" Allwit said.

"Colon" meant "stomach" or "intestines" or "hunger."

His appetite did not care whether the time was Lent.

The first promoter said:

"You say well, sir.

"It is good reason that the colon — the stomach — of a gentleman, as you were lately pleased to term your worship, sir, should be fulfilled and satisfied with answerable — with suitable — food, to sharpen blood, delight health, and tickle nature."

Allwit had called the two promoters "gentlemen," not himself.

"To sharpen blood" means "to increase sexual desire."

"Tickle" means "sexually excite."

The first promoter continued:

"Were you directed here to this street, sir?"

"That I was, aye, by the Virgin Mary," Allwit said.

"And the butcher likely was said to kill and sell close — secretly — in some upper room?" the second promoter asked.

They were hoping to get information from him.

"Some apple loft, as I take it, or a coal house," Allwit said. "I don't know which, indeed."

The second promoter said:

"Either will serve."

The second promoter then said to himself:

"This butcher shall kiss Newgate, unless he turns up the bottom of the pocket of his apron."

Either the butcher would pay the promoters a bribe or he would spend time in Newgate Prison.

Butchers wore aprons.

The second promoter then asked:

"You go to seek him?"

Allwit said:

"Where you shall not find him.

"I'll buy meat and walk by your noses with my flesh, you sheep-biting mongrels, you hand-basket freebooters!"

The promoters raided the food-baskets of passersby.

Allwit continued:

"My wife lies in, resting from giving birth.

"A foutra for promoters!"

"Foutra" refers to sex.

Allwit exited.

The first promoter said after him:

"That shall not serve your turn!"

Pregnant women had cravings, and a husband could be willing to break Lenten regulations against eating meat if his wife craved meat. A 1613 stature forbid the eating of meat during Lent even to most pregnant women and most invalids. Some exemptions existed. No doubt VIPs were exempted; so were those people who bribed the promoters.

News can travel slow, and perhaps some people, including Allwit, were not yet aware of the new law.

Or, possibly, the law had not yet been passed, and the promoter was making an empty threat.

Or, possibly, the law had not yet been passed, and the promoter was threatening to illegally take Allwit's meat.

A Chaste Maid in Cheapside was likely written in 1613.

The first promoter then said:

"What a rogue's this! How cunningly he came over — insulted — us!"

A man entered the scene. He was carrying meat in a basket under his cloak.

"Hush, stand close by and be quiet," the second promoter said.

"I have escaped well thus far," the man with the basket said. "They say the knaves are wondrously hot and busy."

The knaves were the promoters.

"By your leave, sir," the first promoter said, "we must see what you have under your cloak there."

"By your leave, sir" means "with your permission, sir," but the promoters would look in the man's basket with or without permission.

"Have?" the man with the basket said. "I have nothing."

"No, do you tell us that?" the first promoter said. "What makes this lump stick out then? We must see it, sir."

The man with the basket said, "What will you see, sir? A pair of sheets, and two of my wife's foul — dirty — smocks, going to the washers?"

The second promoter said:

"O, we love that sight well. You cannot please us better."

The second promoter had said that the two promoters enjoyed looking at dirty laundry.

He took the basket and opened it.

The second promoter then said:

"What, do you gull us? Are you trying to make fools of us? Do you call these shirts and smocks?"

The man said:

"Now may a pox choke you!"

A pox is 1) a plague, or 2) a venereal disease.

The man continued:

"You have cheated me and five of my wife's kindred of a good dinner; we must make it up now with herrings and milk pottage."

Pottage is broth.

He exited.

"It is all veal," the first promoter said, looking at the meat.

"All veal?" the second promoter said. "Pox, the worse luck. I promised faithfully to send this morning a fat quarter of lamb to a kind gentlewoman in Turnbull Street who longs for it, and now I'm crossed and thwarted."

The kind gentlewoman was probably a pregnant whore.

Turnbull Street was notorious because of its many brothels.

"Let's share this and see what hap — what luck — comes next then," the first promoter said.

Another man with a basket entered the scene.

"Agreed, stand close by and quiet again," the second promoter said. "Here's another booty. Who's he?"

"Sir, by your favor," the first promoter said.

"Meaning me, sir?" the second man said.

"Good Mr. Oliver, I beg thy pardon, indeed," the first promoter said.

The second promoter asked, "What have thou there?"

"A rack — a neck — of mutton, sir, and half a lamb," the second man said. "You know my mistress' diet."

The first promoter said to the second man:

"Go, go, we don't see thee."

He said to the second promoter:

"Keep away from him; keep close by me. By God's heart, let him pass. Thou shall never have the wit to know our benefactors."

Their "benefactors" were people who paid them bribes.

The second man exited.

"I have forgotten him," the second promoter said.

The first promoter said, "It is Mr. Beggarland's serving-man, the wealthy merchant who is in fee with us."

The wealthy merchant had bribed them.

"Now I have a feeling of him," the second promoter said. "I remember him."

"You know he purchased the whole Lent together," the first promoter said. "He gave us ten groats apiece on Ash Wednesday."

The wealthy merchant had paid them for immunity for all of Lent, which began on Ash Wednesday.

Thomas Middleton probably wrote *A Chaste Maid in Cheapside* in 1613; it was published in 1630. In 1613, Ash Wednesday was February 21.

Groats are coins of little value.

"True, true," the second promoter said.

Carrying a basket, the wench who had recently argued with Touchwood Senior entered the scene. No infant could be seen, but in the basket a rump of mutton could be seen.

The first promoter said, "Look! A wench."

"Why, then, stand close by and be quiet indeed," the second promoter said.

The wench said to herself, "Women had need of wit, if they'll shift here, and she who has wit may shift anywhere."

"Shift" can mean 1) succeed, 2) live by committing fraud, and 3) change possession of something from one person to another.

The first promoter said, "Look, look, poor fool, she has left the rump uncovered, too, all the more to betray her. This is like a murderer who will outface the deed with a bloody band — that is, while wearing a bloody collar."

"Outface the deed" means "pretend to be innocent of the murder."

Taking her basket, the second promoter asked the wench, "What time of the year is it, sister?"

"O sweet gentlemen, I am a poor servant," the wench said. "Let me go."

"You shall, wench, but this must stay with us," the first promoter said.

The wench said:

"O, you undo and ruin me, sir. It is for a wealthy gentlewoman who takes medicine, sir. The doctor allows my mistress to eat mutton.

"O, as you tender the dear life of a gentlewoman, I'll bring my master to you, and he shall show you a true authority — a true authorization of exemption from the Lenten regulations — from the higher powers, and I'll run every foot."

"Well, leave your basket then, and run and don't spare any effort to return quickly," the second promoter said.

"Will you swear then to me to keep it until I come back?" the wench asked.

"Now by this light, I will," the first promoter said.

"What do you say, gentleman?" the wench asked the second promoter.

The second promoter said:

"What a strange wench it is.

"I wish that we might perish if we don't keep it until you return."

This was a strong wish — or vow. They would perish everlastingly in Hell if they did not take care of "it."

"Then, I run, sir," the wench said.

She ran away.

"And never return, I hope," the first promoter said.

"A politic baggage — a cunning woman — she makes us swear to keep it," the second promoter said. "I ask you to look what market — what bargain — she has made."

The first promoter said:

"*Imprimis*, sir, a good fat loin of mutton."

Imprimis is Latin for "in the first place."

He then said:

"What comes next under this cloth? I hope now for a quarter of lamb."

The second promoter said, "I hope now for a shoulder of mutton."

"Done," the first promoter said.

The first promoter wanted to bet. He would bet that it was a quarter of lamb, and the second promoter would bet that it was a shoulder of mutton.

"Why 'done,' sir?" the second promoter asked.

Bet? What bet?

The first promoter said, "By the mass, I feel I have lost; it is of more weight, indeed. It weighs more than a quarter of lamb."

The second promoter asked, "Some loin of veal?"

Feeling around in the basket, the first promoter said, "No, indeed, here's a lamb's head, I feel that plainly. Why, yet I'll win my wager."

"Huh?" the second promoter said.

Wager? What wager?

"By God's wounds, what's here?" the first promoter asked, pulling a live infant out of the basket.

"A child!" the second promoter said.

"A pox on all dissembling, cunning whores!" the first promoter said.

"Here's an unlucky breakfast," the second promoter said.

"What shall we do?" the first promoter asked.

"The quean made us swear to keep it, too," the second promoter said.

A "quean" is a whore.

"We might leave it if we had not promised to keep it," the first promoter said.

"This is villainous and strange," the second promoter said. "By God's life, had she no one to gull except poor promoters who watch hard for a living?"

The first promoter said:

"Half our gettings — our earnings — must run in sugar-sops and nurses' wages now, besides many a pound of soap and tallow."

Sugar-sops are pieces of bread that have been soaked in sugar-water.

The first promoter continued:

"We have need to get loins of mutton still, to save suet to use to change to candles so we can watch over the child at night."

Suet is an impure form of tallow, which is used to make candles. The promoters could either exchange the suet for candles, or change the suet into candles.

The second promoter said, "Nothing maddens me except that this was a lamb's head with you. You felt it, and you said that it was the head of a lamb; she has made calves' heads of us."

A "calf" is a fool.

The first promoter said:

"Please say no more about it; there's time to get it up — we have time to get back what we have lost. It is not come to mid-Lent Sunday yet."

Mid-Lent Sunday is the fourth Sunday in Lent. In 1613, the date of Ash Wednesday was March 17. Ash Wednesday is the first day of Lent.

"I am so angry that I'll watch no more today," the second promoter said.

"In faith, nor will I watch," the first promoter said.

"Why, then I'll make a proposal," the second promoter said.

"Well, what is it?" the first promoter asked.

"Let's even go to the Checker Inn at Queenhive and roast the loin of mutton until young flood," the second promoter said, "and then we'll send the child to Brentford."

"Young flood" is the start of the incoming tide.

Many whores lived at Brentford. The promoters could find a wet nurse for the infant there.

They exited.

In a hall in Allwit's house, Allwit was wearing one of Sir Walter Whorehound's suits, and Davy was trussing him: tying the laces of his hose (stockings) to his doublet (jacket).

"It is a busy day at our house, Davy," Allwit said.

"It is always the kursning day, sir," Davy said.

The "kursning day" is the "christening day."

It was always busy on a christening day, and at the Allwits' house, it always seemed to be a christening day.

"Truss, truss me, Davy," Allwit said.

The word "truss" also means "get ready to be hung."

Davy said to himself, "It wouldn't matter if you were hanged, sir."

"How does this suit fit me, Davy?" Allwit asked.

"Excellently and neatly," Davy said. "My master's things were always fit for you, sir, even to a hair, you know."

"My master's things" are 1) my master's clothing, and the "things" can also include 2) my master's penis.

"Even to a hair" means 1) exactly and completely, and 2) right up to the pubic hair.

Davy was saying that Allwit was wearing Sir Walter's suit, which fit him exactly, and he was suggesting that Sir Walter was "wearing" the vagina of Allwit's wife, which fit so well that it provided Allwit with an heir.

Allwit was also "cuckolding" Sir Walter by "wearing" Sir Walter's mistress' vagina, which fit him exactly.

Vaginas tend to be one size fits all.

Allwit said:

"Thou have hit it — guessed it — rightly, Davy. We have ever jumped in one this ten years, Davy. So, well said."

Allwit and Sir Walter Whorehound had 1) been wearing the same clothing for ten years, and/or 2) been sleeping with the same woman for ten years.

Either Allwit had been lying about not sleeping with his wife, or he was now joking.

Carrying a box, a servant entered the scene.

Allwit asked the servant:

"Who are thou?"

"Your comfit-maker's serving-man, sir," the servant said.

A comfit is fruit preserved with sugar.

Allwit said, "O sweet youth, go in to the nurse quickly. Quick, it is time, indeed; your mistress will be here?"

"She was setting forth, sir," the servant said.

The servant exited.

Two Puritans entered the scene.

Allwit said:

"Here come our gossips now. O, I shall have such kissing work today."

"Kissing work" means observing the rules of etiquette.

"Sweet Mistress Underman, welcome, indeed."

Mistress Underman.

Hmm.

Mistress under a man.

The first Puritan said, "May God give you joy of your fine girl, sir, and may God grant that her education may be pure and fitting for one of the faithful."

"I give thanks to you for your sisterly wishes, Mistress Underman," Allwit said.

"Have any of the brethren's wives come yet?" the second Puritan asked.

The brethren are Puritans.

"There are some wives within, and some at home," Allwit said.

"Verily, I give you thanks, sir," the first Puritan — Mistress Underman — said.

The Puritans exited.

Allwit said:

"Verily, you are an ass, indeed.

"I must fit all these times, or there's no music."

He was saying that he had to be agreeable to all the guests, or there would be no music — that is, no harmony and good times.

Two gossips entered the scene.

Allwit said:

"Here comes a friendly and familiar pair. Now I like these wenches well."

"How do thou, sirrah?" the first gossip asked.

"Truly, I am well," Allwit said. "I thank you, neighbor, and how do thou?"

"We want — lack — nothing, but such getting, sir, as is thine," the second gossip said.

The "getting" is 1) income, and/or 2) begetting.

"My gettings, wench, they are poor," Allwit said.

"Fie — bah! — that thou shall say so," the first gossip said. "Thou have as fine children as a man can beget."

Davy said to himself, "Aye, as a man can beget, and that's my master."

His master was Sir Walter Whorehound.

Allwit said:

"They are pretty foolish things, put to making in minutes."

His children were conceived in minutes.

Allwit continued:

"I never stand long about them."

He was never erect and never had a long penis when it came to conceiving the children whom people believed that he fathered.

The other meaning of his sentence is that he did not spend much time with "his" children.

Allwit then asked:

"Will you walk inside, wenches?"

The two gossips exited.

Touchwood Junior and Moll entered the scene.

"This is the happiest meeting that our souls could wish for," Touchwood Junior said. "Here's the ring ready. I am beholden to your father's haste: He has kept his hour."

Yellowhammer had finished the ring when he had said he would.

"He never kept it better," Moll said.

Sir Walter Whorehound entered the scene.

"Stand back," Touchwood Junior said. "Be silent."

He did not want Sir Walter to know that he — that is, Touchwood Junior — and Moll wanted to marry each other.

"Mistress and partner, I will put you both into one cup," Sir Walter Whorehound said.

The mistress was Moll, and the partner was Touchwood Junior.

A mistress is a woman whom one loves.

Touchwood Junior was Sir Walter Whorehound's partner in being godparents.

Sir Walter Whorehound would pledge them both — drink to them both — with one cup of wine.

Davy said to himself:

"Into one cup, most proper …

"A fitting compliment for a goldsmith's daughter."

Allwit said, "Yes, sir, that's the man who must be your worship's partner in this day's business: Mr. Touchwood's brother."

"I embrace your acquaintance, sir," Sir Walter Whorehound said.

"It vows your service, sir," Touchwood Junior said.

"It's near high time," Sir Walter Whorehound said. "Come, Mr. Allwit."

It was time for the christening.

"Ready, sir," Allwit said.

"Will it please you to walk?" Sir Walter Whorehound asked Touchwood Junior.

"Sir, I obey your time," Touchwood Junior said. "I'll follow your lead."

They exited.

— 2.4 —

On the street outside Allwit's house, Maudlin, the gossips, and the Puritans going to the christening talked together. Also present was a midwife, who was holding the baby. They were talking about order of precedence entering the church where the christening would be held. The midwife and infant would go in first, but who should go in second? The person of the highest social class would go in second.

Neither Maudlin nor the first gossip, however, wanted precedence: to go in before the other. They were being humble.

"Good Mrs. Yellowhammer," the first gossip said to Maudlin, offering her precedence.

"In faith, I will not," Maudlin said.

"Indeed, it shall be yours," the first gossip said.

"I have sworn, indeed," Maudlin said.

"I'll stand still then," the first gossip said.

The first gossip would not go in first.

"So you will let the child go without company and make me forsworn," Maudlin said.

Maudlin did not want to go in first.

"You are such another creature," the first gossip said.

She was exasperated — or mock-exasperated. According to her, Maudlin was behaving like an infant.

The midwife and child, Maudlin, and the first gossip exited.

"Before me?" the second gossip said to the third gossip. "I ask you to come down a little. Be a little humbler and take a lower place."

"Not a whit," the third gossip said. "I hope I know my place."

The second gossip and the third gossip each wanted to enter the christening room before the other.

"Your place?" the second gossip said. "That would be a great wonder, to be sure! Are you any better than a comfit-maker's wife?"

A comfit-maker is a confectioner.

"And that's as good at all times as an apothecary's wife," the third gossip said.

The second gossip was an apothecary's wife, and the third gossip was a comfit-maker's wife.

"Ye lie, yet I forbear you, too," the second gossip said.

The second gossip refrained from doing something unpleasant to the third gossip.

The second and third gossips exited.

The first Puritan said to the second Puritan, "Come, sweet sister, we go in unity, and show the fruits of peace like children of the spirit."

"I love lowliness," the second Puritan said.

The Puritans exited.

The fourth gossip said, "True, and so say I; although they strive more, there comes as proud behind as goes before."

The Puritans were proud of their humility.

"Proud" can mean "sexually excited."

"Comes as proud behind" may refer to anal sex.

"Every inch, indeed," the fifth gossip said.

They exited.

CHAPTER 3

— 3.1 —

Touchwood Junior and a parson talked together in a church.

"O sir, if ever you felt the force of love, pity it in me," Touchwood Junior said.

"Yes, although I never was married, sir, I have felt the force of love from good men's daughters, and some who will be maidens yet three years hence," the parson said. "Have you got a license?"

The parson was hinting that he had had love affairs, including with some women whom he had given certificates that they were virgins of good character.

"Here," Touchwood Junior said. "It is ready, sir."

"That's well," the parson said.

"The ring and all things perfect, she'll steal hither," Touchwood Junior said.

"She shall be welcome, sir," the parson said. "I'll not be long a-clapping you together."

He would quickly marry them.

Moll and Touchwood Senior entered the scene.

"O, here she's come, sir," Touchwood Junior said.

"Who's he?" the parson asked.

"My honest brother," Touchwood Junior said.

"Quick, make haste, sirs," Touchwood Senior said.

"You must dispatch with all the speed you can, for I shall be missed straightaway," Moll said. "I made hard shift for this small time I have. It was hard work to get away for a short time."

The parson said:

"Then I'll not linger; place that ring upon her finger."

Touchwood Junior placed the wedding ring on Moll's finger.

The parson then said:

"This the finger plays the part, whose master vein shoots from the heart."

In this society, many people believed that a vein connected the ring finger of the left hand to the heart.

The parson then said:

"Now join hands —"

Holding hands — handfasting — was a part of the betrothal and of the wedding ceremony.

As the priest said these words, Yellowhammer and Sir Walter Whorehound entered the scene.

Yellowhammer interrupted, "— which I will sever, and so never again shall these hands meet, never."

"O, we are betrayed!" Moll said.

"Hard fate!" Touchwood Junior said.

"I am struck with wonder," Sir Walter Whorehound said.

Yellowhammer said to Moll, his daughter:

"Was this the politic fetch — the cunning trick — thou mystical baggage, thou disobedient strumpet?"

"Mystical" means "secret."

Yellowhammer then said to Sir Walter Whorehound, "And were you so wise to send for her to such an end?"

Sir Walter Whorehound replied, "Now I disclaim the end — you'll make me mad."

Sir Walter Whorehound had invited Moll to the christening; now Yellowhammer was wondering if he did that to help Moll get married to someone else. Of course, Sir Walter denied that he had done that. In fact, he wanted to marry Moll.

"And who are you, sir?" Yellowhammer asked Touchwood Junior.

"If you cannot see with those two glasses, put on an additional pair," Touchwood Junior said.

Yellowhammer said:

"I dreamt of anger always."

He had always dreamed about being angry and imagined what it would be like, but now he really was angry. Or perhaps he had had a premonitory dream.

He then said to Touchwood Junior:

"Here, take your ring, sir."

He took the wedding ring off Moll's hand.

Looking at the ring, he said:

"Ha, this ring? By God's life, it is the same: abominable! Didn't I sell this ring?"

"I think you did," Touchwood Junior said. "You received money for it."

Yellowhammer said, "By God's heart, listen, knight, here's 'no' unconscionable villainy — he set me to work to make the wedding ring, and he came with an intent to steal my daughter. Did ever any runaway match it?"

He gave Touchwood Junior the wedding ring he had paid for.

"Is this man your brother, sir?" Sir Walter Whorehound asked Touchwood Senior.

"He can tell that as well as I can," Touchwood Senior said.

Yellowhammer said to Touchwood Junior:

"The very posy mocks me to my face: 'Love that's wise, blinds parents' eyes.'

"I thank your wisdom, sir, for the blinding of us; we have good hope to recover our sight shortly. In the meantime, I will lock up this baggage as carefully as I lock up my gold; she shall see as little sun as my gold sees if a close room or something similar can keep her from the light of it."

"O sweet father, for love's sake, pity me!" Moll said.

"Away!" Yellowhammer said.

Moll said to Touchwood Junior, "Farewell, sir, may all content bless thee, and take this for comfort: Although violence may keep me here, thou can lose me never, I am always thine although we part forever."

"Aye, we shall part you, minx," Yellowhammer said.

Yellowhammer and Moll exited.

"Your acquaintance, sir, came very recently, yet it came too soon," Sir Walter said. "I must hereafter know you for no friend, but as one whom I must shun like pestilence, or the disease of lust."

"Likely enough, sir, you have taken me at the worst time for words that ever you picked out," Touchwood Junior said. "In faith, do not wrong me, sir."

Touchwood Junior did not want to be underestimated.

Touchwood Junior and the parson exited.

Touchwood Senior said:

"Look after him — beware of him — and don't spare him; there walks a man who never yet received and patiently endured baffling and public humiliation; you're blessed more than anyone I ever knew."

Sir Walter Whorehound was blessed because Touchwood Junior had not killed him.

Touchwood Senior concluded:

"Go take your rest."

Touchwood Senior exited.

Sir Walter Whorehound said to himself, "I pardon you; you Touchwoods are both losers."

A proverb stated, "Give losers leave to speak."

Sir Walter Whorehound was ignoring the threat.

He exited.

In Allwit's house, Allwit's wife lay in bed after giving birth.

All the gossips, including Maudlin and Lady Kix, entered the room, as did the wet nurse, who was carrying the newborn.

The first gossip asked Allwit's wife, "How are things, woman? We have brought you home a kursen soul."

"Kursen" means "Christian."

"Aye, I thank your pains," Mistress Allwit said.

"And verily well kursened, in the right way, without idolatry or superstition, after the pure manner of Amsterdam," the first Puritan said.

Amsterdam was a place of religious tolerance; many Puritans lived there.

The baby had been christened in a manner approved by Puritans.

"Kursened" means "christened."

Mistress Allwit said:

"Sit down, good neighbors."

She then called:

"Nurse!"

"Here I am, already at hand, indeed," the wet nurse said.

"Look and make sure that they all have low stools to sit on," Mistress Allwit said.

Puritans liked lowliness.

"They have, indeed," the wet nurse said.

The second gossip said:

"Bring the child hither, nurse."

The wet nurse came over to her with the child.

The second gossip then said to the third gossip:

"What do you say now, gossip? Isn't it a chopping — a vigorous — girl, so like the father?"

The third gossip said:

"As if it had been spit out of his mouth."

She was saying that the girl was the spitting image of Allwit; however, Allwit's semen had produced the child exactly as much as his spit had.

The third gossip continued:

"She is eyed, nosed, and browed as like him as a girl can be. Only indeed the infant has the mother's mouth."

"The mother's mouth up and down, up and down," the second gossip said.

"Up and down" means "exactly." But it also means that mother's lips go up and down and that the baby girl is exactly like the mother when it comes to her mouth and vagina.

"It is a large child, she's just a little woman," the third gossip said about the infant.

The second person said about the infant, "Believe me, she is a very spiny creature, but she is all heart, well mettled, like the faithful to endure her tribulation here, and raise up seed."

"Spiny" means 1) lean, and/or 2) resembling a thorn, and "mettled" means 1) courageous, and/or 2) amorous.

"The child had a sore labor of it, I promise you; you can tell, neighbor," the second gossip said.

The third gossip said:

"O, she had great speed — great success. We were afraid once, but she made us all have joyful hearts again."

In this society, many infants died while being born.

The third gossip continued:

"It is a good soul, indeed. The midwife found her a most cheerful daughter."

"It is the spirit," the first Puritan said. "The sisters are all like her."

This kind of spirit may be the Holy Spirit.

Or the spirit may be alcohol, which makes people cheerful.

Sir Walter Whorehound entered the room with two spoons and plate and with Allwit.

Spoons and plate (gold or gold-plated ware, or silver or silver-plated ware) were traditional christening gifts.

The female gossips talked quietly among themselves about Sir Walter.

"O, here comes the chief gossip, neighbors," the second gossip said.

Sir Walter was the chief godparent and gossip. Moll was an additional godparent and gossip. She was not present.

"The fatness — the richest part — of your wishes to you all, ladies," Sir Walter Whorehound said.

"O dear sweet gentleman, what fine words he has — the fatness of our wishes,'" the third gossip said.

"He calls us all ladies," the second gossip said.

"I promise you that he is a fine and courteous gentleman," the fourth gossip said.

"I think that her husband seems like a clown — a peasant or country bumpkin— compared to him," the second gossip said.

"I would not care what clown my husband were, too, as long as I had such fine children," the third gossip said.

"She has all fine children, gossip," the second gossip agreed.

"Aye, and see how fast they come," the third gossip said.

"Children are blessings, if they are begotten with zeal, by the brethren, as I have five at home," the First Puritan said.

The zeal may be 1) religious zeal, and/or 2) sexual zeal.

The First Puritan has five children at home? Whole lotta zeal going on.

"The worst is past, I hope, now, gossip," Sir Walter said.

The time of greatest danger that Mistress Allwit would die of complications from childbirth were over, he hoped.

"So I hope, too, good sir," Mistress Allwit said.

She also hoped that the time of greatest danger that the infant would die was over.

"Why then so hope I, too, for company," Allwit said. "I have nothing to do else."

He was willing to join those present in hoping that his wife and the infant would not die.

Sir Walter gave Mistress Allwit a cup and spoons and said, "A poor remembrance, lady! I pray that you accept this gift to the love of the babe."

"O, you are at too much charge, sir," Mistress Allwit said.

These were expensive christening gifts.

"Look, look at what has he given her," the second gossip said. "What is it, gossip?"

The third gossip said, "Now by my faith, a fair high standing cup, and two great apostle spoons, one of them gilt."

A standing cup is a goblet with a stem.

"Gilt" here means "silver coated with gold." The other spoon was silver.

Apostle spoons were spoons whose handles were the figure of an apostle.

"Surely that was Judas then with the red beard," the first Puritan said.

She had heard "gilt" and thought that "guilt" was meant.

Traditionally, Judas had a red beard.

As the betrayer of Christ, Judas is a poor choice of an apostle to adorn a christening spoon.

Red hair was associated with licentiousness.

The second Puritan said, "I would not feed my daughter with that spoon for all the world, for fear of coloring her hair. The brethren do not like red hair; it consumes them much. It is not the sisters' color."

Red hair consumed Puritans with sexual passion, and it consumed them with anger because they dislike it so much.

The dry nurse brought comfits and wine into the room.

Allwit said:

"Well done, nurse. Go about, about with them among the gossips."

He then said to himself:

"Now out comes all the tasseled handkerchiefs. They are spread abroad between their knees already. Now in goes the long fingers that are washed some three times a day in urine — my wife uses it."

Urine was regarded as a cleansing liquid.

Allwit continued saying to himself:

"Now we shall have such pocketing."

Some of the comfits vanished into pockets to be taken home and eaten.

Allwit continued saying to himself:

"See how they lurch at the lower end."

At the lower end of the table, the gossips were eating more and pocketing more than their fair share of the food. If this was a contest between the lower end and the higher end, the lower end was winning.

The higher end of the table was for the gossips with the higher social status.

Many Puritans, who loved lowliness, had big appetites. That would keep their lower end busy the next day.

"Come here, nurse," the first Puritan said to the dry nurse going around and serving the food.

"Again!" Allwit said to himself. "She has taken food twice already."

"I had forgotten a sister's child who is sick," the first Puritan said.

She was saying that she wanted to take comfits to the ill child.

Allwit said to himself:

"A pox, it seems your purity loves sweet things well that puts in thrice together."

The first Puritan loved sweet things; this was her third time taking food.

Allwit continued saying to himself:

"Had this been all at my expense now, I had been beggared.

"These women have no consciences at sweetmeats, wherever they come; see if they have not culled — picked — out all the long sugarplums, too — they have left nothing here but short wriggle-tail — that is, tiny — comfits, not worth mouthing."

The gossips preferred long sugarplums — metaphorically, they preferred long penises.

The gossips rejected short wriggle-tails — metaphorically, they rejected short penises, which were not worth mouthing.

Long, erect penises do not wriggle.

Allwit continued saying to himself:

"It's no marvel that I heard a citizen complain once that his wife's belly alone broke his back."

His wife's appetite for food (and sex) had broken the citizen's back through overwork.

Allwit continued saying to himself:

"My back would have been all in fitters — in tatters — seven years since, except for this worthy knight who with a prop upholds my wife and me, and all my estate would have been buried in Bucklersbury."

Many grocers sold their wares on Bucklersbury Street.

"Here, Mistress Yellowhammer, and neighbors, to you all who have taken pains with me, all the good wives at once," Mistress Allwit said.

She wanted to drink a toast to them.

"I'll answer for them," the first Puritan said. "They all wish for health and strength and that you may courageously go forward, to perform the like and many such, like a true sister with motherly bearing."

Allwit said to himself, "Now the cups troll about — are passed around — to wet the gossips' whistles. The wine pours down, indeed: they never think of payment."

"Fill my cup again, nurse," the first Puritan said.

Allwit said to himself:

"Now bless thee, two at once. I'll stay no longer. It would kill me if I paid for it."

He asked Sir Walter:

"Will it please you to walk downstairs and leave the women?"

"With all my heart, Jack," Sir Walter Whorehound said.

"Truly, I cannot blame you," Allwit said.

"All of you, sit, merry ladies," Sir Walter said.

"Thank your worship, sir," one of the gossips said.

"Thank your worship, sir," the first Puritan said.

"May a pox twice tipple you," Allwit said to himself. "You are last and lowest."

The first Puritan had been doing a lot of tippling. Excessive tippling often results in toppling.

Allwit wanted the first Puritan to suffer from the pox — the plague or a venereal disease — twice.

Allwit and Sir Walter exited the scene.

"Bring here that same cup, Nurse," the first Puritan said. "I would like to drive away this — hic! — anti-Christian grief."

She drank.

Psalm 104:15 states, in part, that *wine [...] maketh glad the heart of man* (King James Version).

"See, gossip, if she doesn't lie in like a countess," the third gossip said about Mistress Allwit. "I wish that I had such a husband for my daughter."

Mistress Allwit's hospitality was very good — like the hospitality that a countess could afford.

"Isn't your daughter interested in marriage?" the fourth gossip asked.

"O no, sweet gossip," the third gossip said.

"Why, she's nineteen!" the fourth gossip said.

"Aye, that she was last Lammas, but she has a fault, gossip, a secret fault," the third gossip said.

Lammas is August 1. It was the time of a harvest festival.

"A fault?" the fourth gossip said. "What is it?"

One kind of "fault" is a vulva.

"I'll tell you when I have drunk more wine," the third gossip said.

"Wine can do that, I see, which friendship cannot," the fourth gossip said to herself.

Wine — that is, drunkenness — can make someone tell secrets.

The third gossip drank and said, "And now I'll tell you, gossip — she's too free."

"Is free" can mean 1) is incontinent, and/or 2) is licentious: sexually active.

"Too free?" the fourth gossip said.

"O aye, she cannot lie dry in her bed," the third gossip said.

The wetness can come from 1) peeing the bed, or 2) making a wet spot during sex.

"What, and nineteen?" the fourth gossip said.

"It is as I tell you, gossip," the third gossip said.

A nurse entered the scene and spoke to Maudlin.

"Someone wants to speak with me, nurse?" Maudlin asked. "Who is it?

"A gentleman from Cambridge," the nurse said. "I think it is your son, indeed."

"It is my son, Tim, indeed. Please call him to come up here among the women," Maudlin said. "It will embolden him well, for he wants — lacks —nothing but audacity. I wish that the Welsh gentlewoman at home were here now."

The nurse exited to get Tim.

"Has your son come, truly?" Lady Kix asked.

"Yes, from the university, truly," Maudlin said.

"It is a great joy to you," Lady Kix said.

"There's a great marriage towards — that is, anticipated — for him," Maudlin said.

"A marriage?" Lady Kix asked.

"Yes, to be sure, a huge heir in Wales, at least to nineteen mountains, besides her goods and cattle," Maudlin said.

Her son, Tim, entered the scene.

Seeing all the women, he said, "O, I'm betrayed!"

Tim had not expected to be the only man among so many women.

He exited, quickly.

Maudlin said:

"What! Gone again?

"Run after him, good nurse."

The dry nurse exited.

Maudlin then said:

"He's so bashful; that's the spoil of youth. In the university they're kept always among men, and they are never trained up in how to be women's company."

"Spoil" means "ruination."

"It is a great spoil of youth indeed," Lady Kix said.

The dry nurse returned with Tim.

"Your mother will have it so," the dry nurse said to Tim.

Maudlin said, "Why, son! Why, Tim! What! Must I rise and fetch you? For shame, son."

Tim said:

"Mother, you do entreat like a freshwoman."

A freshwoman would be a first-year female university student, but at the time Tim's university did not admit women as students. Tim meant by "freshwoman" a female naïve person.

Tim continued:

"It is against the laws of the university for any who has completed the requirements for a bachelor's degree to thrust among married wives."

"Thrust" has a sexual connotation, but Tim meant "to be thrust into the company of wives."

A person who has completed the requirements for a bachelor's degree ought to know that the phrase "married wives" is wordy.

"Come, we'll excuse you here," Maudlin said.

"Call up my tutor, mother, and I don't mind staying here," Tim said.

If his tutor was OK with being among a number of wives, then so would Tim be OK with it.

"What!" Maudlin said. "Has your tutor come? Have you brought him up here?"

Tim said:

"I have not brought him up here."

Maudlin meant "brought him up to London" in her question, but Tim meant "brought him upstairs" in his reply.

Tim continued:

"He is standing at the door. *Negatur*, there's logic to begin with you, mother."

Negatur was a Latin phrase used in argumentation: "It is denied."

Maudlin said:

"Run, call the gentleman, nurse; he's my son's tutor."

The dry nurse exited.

She then said to Tim:

"Here, eat some sugarplums."

"I come from Cambridge, and you offer me six sugarplums?" Tim asked.

His mother was treating him like a child.

Maudlin asked, "Why, what is this now, Tim? Won't your old tricks yet be left?"

"Should I be treated like a child, when I have fulfilled the requirements for a bachelor's degree?" Tim replied.

"You'll never lin — cease or learn — until I make your tutor whip you," Maudlin said. "You know how I served you once at the free school in St. Paul's churchyard?"

Tim said, "O monstrous absurdity! Never was the like in Cambridge since my time. By God's life, whip a bachelor? You'd be laughed at soundly! Don't let my tutor hear you: It would be a jest throughout the whole university. Say no more words about that, mother."

Tim's tutor entered the scene.

"Is this your tutor, Tim?" Maudlin asked.

"Yes, surely, lady," the tutor said. "I am the man who brought him in league with logic and read the Dunces to him."

The Dunces are the writings of the philosopher-theologian Duns Scotus.

Dunces are also fools.

"That he did, mother, but now I have them all in my own pate — my own head — and I can as well read them to others," Tim said.

"That he can, mistress, for they flow naturally from him," the tutor said.

A "natural" is a born fool.

"I'm the more beholden to your pains, sir," Maudlin said.

"*Non ideo sane*," the tutor said.

["Not indeed on that account."]

Maudlin, who thought that *ideo* meant "idiot," said:

"True, he was an idiot indeed when he went out of London, but now he's well mended.

"Did you receive the two goose pies I sent you?"

Readers may be forgiven for thinking of two gooses, aka fools: Tim and his tutor.

"Yes, and I ate them heartily, thanks to your worship," the tutor said.

"This is my son, Tim," Maudlin said. "I ask you to bid him welcome, gentlewomen."

Tim said, "Tim? Listen, call me Timotheus, mother — Timotheus."

"What!" Maudlin said. "Shall I deny your name? 'Timotheus,' said he? Indeed, there's a name! This is my son, Tim, truly."

"You're welcome, Mr. Tim," Lady Kix said.

She kissed him.

Tim said:

"O, this is horrible. She wets as she kisses.

"Use your handkerchief, sweet tutor, to wipe the kisses off as fast as they come on."

"Welcome back from Cambridge," the second gossip said.

She kissed him.

Tim said:

"This is intolerable! This woman would have a villainous sweet breath if she didn't stink of comfits!

"Help me, sweet tutor, or I shall rub my lips off."

"I'll go kiss the lower end for a while," the tutor said.

He meant those women sitting at the lower end of the table and not what they were sitting on.

"Perhaps that's the sweeter," Tim said, "and we shall dispatch — finish — the sooner."

Tim meant "the sweeter idea," but readers may be forgiven if they thought he meant that the women's lower ends smelled sweeter than their breaths.

"Let me come next," the first Puritan said. "Welcome from the wellspring of discipline that waters all the brethren."

Drunk, she reeled and fell.

"Hoist her, I beg thee!" Tim said. "Help her up!"

The third gossip said, "O, bless the woman — Mistress Underman!"

"It is but the common affliction of the faithful," the First Puritan said. "We must embrace our falls."

According to Calvinist doctrine, Humankind must accept its fallen state.

Tim said, "I'm glad I escaped her kiss. It was some rotten kiss surely. She dropped down before her kiss came at me."

Allwit and Davy entered the scene.

Allwit said to Davy:

"Here's a noise! They are not departed yet! Heyday, a looking glass!"

The first Pilgrim was still lying on the floor. Allwit was sarcastically asking for a mirror he could use to see if she was breathing.

"Looking glass" was also slang for a chamber pot.

Allwit then added:

"They have drunk so hard in plate that some of them had need of other vessels."

"In plate" were drinking vessels.

Other vessels were chamber-pots to pee in.

Allwit then said:

"Yonder's the bravest — the most splendid — show."

"Where?" all the gossips asked. "Where, sir?"

"Come along immediately by the Pissing Conduit, with two brave drums and a standard bearer," Allwit said.

The conduit's steam of water resembled a stream of urine.

"Two brave drums and a standard bearer?"

Hmm.

Two testicles and an erect penis.

"O, brave!" all the gossips said. "Splendid!"

The phallic image excited them.

"Come, tutor," Tim said.

"Farewell, sweet gossip," all the gossips said to Mistress Allwit.

"I thank you all for your pains," Mistress Allwit said.

"Eat and grow strong," the first Puritan said.

Everyone except Allwit, Davy, and Mistress Allwit exited.

Allwit said to his wife:

"You had more need to sleep than eat."

When someone is sleeping, that person is not committing adultery.

Allwit continued:

"Go, take a nap with some of the brethren, go, and rise up a well-edified, boldified sister."

The brethren were drunk and needed to sleep it off.

Allwit then drew the thick curtains around his wife's bed so she could sleep without being disturbed by noise.

Allwit then said to Davy:

"O, here's a day of toil well passed over, able to make a citizen hare-mad."

Hares grow madder — wilder — in the mating season.

Allwit continued:

"How hot they have made the room with their thick bums! Don't thou feel it, Davy?"

"The heat is monstrously strong, sir," Davy said.

"What's here under the stools?" Allwit asked.

"Nothing but wet, sir," Davy said. "Probably, some wine spilt here."

Allwit said:

"Is it no worse, do thou think?"

Urine would be worse than spilled wine.

"Fair needlework stools cost them nothing, Davy."

He was wondering if the needlework stools had been damaged. These stools were padded — thus, the needlework.

"Nor with you, either, indeed," Davy said to himself.

The stools cost Allwit nothing: Sir Walter paid for them.

Allwit said:

"Look how they have laid the stools down — even as they lie themselves, with their heels up."

"Heels up" meant "ready for sex."

Allwit continued:

"How they have shuffled up the rushes, too, Davy, with their short, figging, little, shittle-cork heels."

The gossips were wearing heels made with cork.

"Shittle-cork" means "shuttle-cock," which goes back and forth in the game of shuttlecock.

Figuratively, think of a woman going back and forth from one cock to another.

Rushes, or rush mats, were strewn or placed on the floors of houses.

"Figging" can be an insulting word. A "fig" is an obscene gesture.

"Figging" can mean 1) fidgeting, or 2) f**king.

Allwit continued:

"These women can let nothing stand as they find it."

Including erections.

Allwit then asked:

"But what's the secret thou were about to tell me, my honest Davy?"

Davy began, "If you should disclose it, sir —"

Allwit interrupted, "— by God's life, rip my belly up to the throat then, Davy."

"My master's set upon marriage," Davy said. "He wants to get married."

"Marriage, Davy?" Allwit said. "Send me to hanging rather."

If Sir Walter Whorehound got married, he would no longer support Allwit's household. This would be a serious financial blow for Allwit. Allwit would rather be hung than lose that financial support.

"I have stung him," Davy said to himself.

Allwit asked, "When? Where? Who is she, Davy?"

"Even the same woman who was the gossip and gave the christening spoon," Davy said.

Moll was the gossip. Sir Walter Whorehound wanted to marry her.

"I have no time to stay, nor scarcely can I speak," Allwit said. "I'll stop those wheels, or all the work will break."

He exited.

Alone, Davy said to himself:

"I knew it would prick him.

"Thus do I fashion always all my own ends by him and his rank toil. It is my desire to keep Sir Walter always away from marriage. Being his poor nearest kinsman, I may fare the better at his death. There my hopes build since my Lady Kix is dry — barren — and she has no child."

Davy was looking out for himself. He was Sir Walter's closest relative, and if Sir Walter died without an heir, Davy would inherit the property. If the Kixes had no heir, and if Sir Walter had no heir, Davy would inherit the wealth of Sir Walter *and* the Kixes.

Davy exited.

— 3.3 —

The Touchwoods, Senior and Junior, talked together in Sir Oliver Kix' house.

Touchwood Junior said to his older brother:

"You are in the happiest way to enrich yourself and give me pleasure, brother, as man's feet can tread in, for although Moll is locked up, her vow is fixed only to me. So then time shall never grieve me, for by that vow, even absent I enjoy her, assuredly confirmed that no one else shall, which will make tedious years seem gameful — joyful and sexually active — to me.

"In the mean space — that is, in the meantime — lose no time, sweet brother. You have the means to strike at this knight's fortunes and lay him level with his bankrupt merit."

Touchwood Junior did not respect Sir Oliver Kix. He regarded him as paying Touchwood Senior to cuckold him so that his wife would get pregnant and conceive an heir. Thus, Sir Oliver's merit was bankrupt.

Or, possibly, he was also referring to Sir Walter Whorehound, whose merit was also bankrupt. Touchwood Senior could get Lady Kix pregnant with an heir with the result that Sir Walter would not be able to inherit the wealth of the Kixes. That would be Touchwood Junior's revenge on Sir Walter.

Touchwood Junior continued:

"Just get his wife pregnant, perch at tree top, and shake the golden fruit into her lap."

The image was that of a harvester climbing a fruit tree and shaking it so that the fruit would fall into the lap of a woman holding out her apron.

The Garden of the Hesperides, who were nymphs of the evening, had golden fruits. One of Hercules' famous labors was to get some of the golden apples of the garden.

Danaë was impregnated by a golden shower that the god Jupiter had turned himself into.

The fruit — a child — would be golden because the Kixes would have an heir to inherit their property.

Touchwood Junior continued:

"Go about it, before she weeps herself to a dry ground and whines out all her goodness."

In other words: Set about getting her pregnant before she becomes barren — too old to have children — and weeps.

Weeping could dry her out and make her barren through loss of water in her tears.

Touchwood Senior said:

"Please cease. I find too much aptness in my blood for such a business without provocation.

"You might well have spared this banquet of eringoes, artichokes, potatoes, and buttered crab; they were fitter kept for your own wedding dinner."

Eringoes are candied roots of sea holly.

All the foods mentioned, including sweet potatoes, were considered aphrodisiacs.

The Touchwoods had eaten a meal together.

Touchwood Junior said:

"Nay, if you'll follow my suit, you'll save my purse, too."

He meant love suit. He still hoped to have Moll, and with her, her dowry.

Men kept their money in a container they called a purse.

Touchwood Junior continued:

"Fortune dotes on me; a man is in a happy case when he finds such an honest friend in the common place."

The word "case" could mean 1) vagina, or 2) law case.

His older brother could help Touchwood Junior make Moll's case happy.

The common place is literally the Court of Common Pleas.

Figuratively, a man is lucky to find an honest friend when he needs one. Touchwood Junior needed an honest friend, and his older brother was such a friend to him.

"By God's life, what makes thee so merry?" Touchwood Senior said. "Thou have no reason to be merry that I could hear of recently since thy crosses and setbacks unless news has come, with new additional details."

Touchwood Junior's wedding to Moll had recently been prevented. Why, then, was he so happy?

"Why, there thou have it right," Touchwood Junior said. "I look for her this evening, brother."

He was expecting to see Moll that night.

This was news to Touchwood Senior.

"What's that?" Touchwood Senior said. "Look for her?"

Touchwood Junior said:

"I will tell you about the wonder straightaway, brother.

"By the firm secrecy and kind assistance of a good wench in the house, who, made of pity, weighing the case her own, Moll is being led through gutters, strange hidden ways, which none but love could find, or have the heart to venture."

Readers will learn that the good wench is Susan, Moll's chambermaid.

The gutters were roof gutters. Susan was guiding Moll over rooftops.

Touchwood Junior continued:

"I expect her where you would little think I would see her."

"I don't care where you see her, as long as she is safe, and yours," Touchwood Senior said.

"Hope tells me so, but from your love and time, my peace must grow," Touchwood Junior said.

He exited.

Touchwood Senior said:

"You know the worst then, brother. Things can only get better.

"Now to my Kixes, the barren he and she; they're in the next room. But to say which of their two humors hold them now at this instant, I cannot say truly."

Their two humors — moods or dispositions — were 1) quarrelsome, and 2) loving. They would quarrel, and then they would kiss and become friends again. The Kixes did this again and again, all day long.

In the next room, Sir Oliver Kix said to his Lady Kix, "Thou lie, barrenness."

He was loud enough that Touchwood Senior could hear him.

Touchwood Senior now knew that they were in a quarreling humor, aka mood.

He said:

"O, is it that time of day? May God give you joy of your tongue — there's nothing else good in you."

Touchwood Senior hoped that Sir Oliver got joy from his tongue; he did not get joy from his penis.

He continued:

"This is their life the whole day from eyes open to eyes shut, kissing or scolding, and then after scolding, they must be made friends. Then they rail out the second part of the first fit of anger, and then they must be pleased again — no man knows which way they act and which mood they will be in."

A "fit" is also a part of a song.

The Kixes metaphorically kept singing the same song all day.

Touchwood Senior continued:

"They fall out like giants, and fall in like children —

"Their fruit can witness as much."

Their quarrels seem significant, like those of giants.

"Fall in" can mean 1) make up, or 2) have sex.

Children easily become friends, but they don't have fruit: children and heirs.

Sir Oliver Kix and Lady Kix entered the scene.

"It is thy fault," Sir Oliver said to his wife.

"Mine, drought and coldness?" Lady Kix replied.

"It is thine," Sir Oliver said. "The problem is that thou are barren."

Lady Kix said, "I barren! O by God's life, that I dared just to speak now, in my own justice, in my own right — I barren! It was otherwise with me when I was at court. I was never called so until I was married."

"I'll be divorced," Sir Oliver said.

Divorce was a difficult process.

"Be hanged!" Lady Kix said. "I need not wish it — that will come too soon to thee. I may say that marriage and hanging go by destiny, for all the goodness I can find in marriage yet."

"I'll give up house, and keep some fruitful whore, like an old bachelor in a tradesman's chamber," Sir Oliver said. "She and her children shall have all."

"Where are they?" Lady Kix asked.

She did not believe they existed. Sir Oliver had trouble making women pregnant.

"Please, cease," Touchwood Senior said. "When there are friendlier courses taken for you to beget and multiply within your house, at your own proper — personal — costs in spite of censure, I think an honest peace might be established."

The Kixes had made arrangements to get an heir, but society could criticize those arrangements.

"What!" Sir Oliver said. "With her? Never."

"Sweet sir," Touchwood Senior said.

"You work all in vain," Sir Oliver replied.

"Then he does all like thee," Lady Kix said.

Sir Oliver sometimes succeeded in having sex with Lady Kix, but the sex did not result in children. He "worked" in vain. So far, Touchwood Senior had not gotten Lady Kix pregnant, but he had not had time to "work."

Touchwood Senior attempted to make peace between the Kixes, but his attempts did not result in peace.

"Let me entreat, sir," Touchwood Senior said.

"May singleness confound her," Sir Oliver said. "I took her with one smock."

After divorce, Lady Kix would be single.

When Sir Oliver had married Lady Kix, she had little property.

"But indeed, you came not so single, when you came from shipboard," Lady Kix said.

"Single" means "unaccompanied." In this society, lice were a problem. Sir Oliver may have been accompanied by many lice, which bite and feed on blood. Or he may have had a woman with him.

"By God's heart, she bit sore there," Sir Oliver said to Touchwood Senior. "Please, make us friends."

"Has it come to that?" Touchwood Senior said. "The peal begins to cease."

"Peal" means "cannon fire" or the sound of an alarm bell.

"I'll sell all at an outcry," Sir Oliver said.

An "outcry" is an auction.

Lady Kix said to her husband:

"Do thy worst, slave."

She then said to Touchwood Senior.

"Good, sweet sir, bring us into love again."

"Some would think this impossible to compass and accomplish," Touchwood Senior said. "Please, let this storm fly over."

"Good sir, pardon me, I'm master of this house, which I'll sell immediately," Sir Oliver said. "I'll clap up bills this evening."

The bills would be posters advertising that the house was for sale.

"Lady, will you be friends with him?" Touchwood Senior said. "Come."

Lady Kix said:

"If ever you loved a woman, don't talk about it, sir.

"What! Be friends with him? In good faith, do you think I'm mad? With one who's scarcely the hinder quarter of a man?"

The hinder quarter is the rear part, not the part that includes the penis.

Lady Kix was saying that her husband had the back part of a man but was lacking in the front area.

"Thou are nothing of a woman," Sir Oliver said.

A "thing" can be a penis. As a woman, Lady Kix had "no thing."

"I wish that I were less than nothing," Lady Kix said.

She wept.

"Please tell me what thou mean?" Sir Oliver asked.

"I cannot please you," Lady Kix said.

She meant that she could not please him in bed.

"Indeed, thou are a good soul," Sir Oliver said. "He lies who says that you cannot please me. Buss, buss, pretty rogue."

"Buss" means "kiss."

"You don't care for me," Lady Kix said.

"Can any man tell now which way they came in?" Touchwood Senior said. "By this light, I'll be hanged then if any man can tell that."

Now the Kixes were becoming all lovey-dovey, but when they came into the room, they were quarreling.

"Has the drink come?" Sir Oliver asked.

Touchwood Senior said:

"Here's a little vial —"

He then said to himself:

"— of almond-milk that cost me some three pence."

"I hope to see thee, wench, within these few years, encircled by children, dressing up a girl and putting jewels in the children's little ears," Sir Oliver said. "That would be fine entertainment, indeed."

"Aye, had you been anything, husband," Lady Kix said, "it had been done before this time."

"Had I been anything!" Sir Oliver said. "Hang thee, had thou been anything. But I have always found thee to be a cross thing."

"Thou are a grub to say so," Lady Kix said.

"A pox on thee," Sir Oliver said.

Touchwood Senior said:

"By this light, they are out again at the same door, and no man can tell which way they will go."

The Kixes had returned to quarreling. Would they continue to quarrel for a while, or would they immediately become lovey-dovey?

Touchwood Senior then said:

"Come, here's your drink, sir."

"I will not take it now, sir, even if I were sure to beget three boys before midnight," Sir Oliver said.

"Why, there thou show now of what breed thou come!" Lady Kix said. "To hinder generation! O thou villain, who knows how crookedly the world goes with us for lack of heirs, yet thou put by all good fortune."

They needed an heir, yet now Sir Oliver was refusing to beget one.

"Hang, strumpet, I will take it now in spite," Sir Oliver said.

"After drinking it, you must then ride for five hours," Touchwood Senior said.

This would get Sir Oliver out of the way while Touchwood Senior "treated" Lady Kix.

Sir Oliver said:

"I intend to."

He then called:

"Who is within there?"

A servant entered the scene and said, "Sir?"

Sir Oliver ordered:

"Saddle the white mare."

He then said:

"I'll take a whore along, and ride to Ware."

Ware was twenty miles north of London. It was a popular location for assignations.

"Ride to the devil," Lady Kix said.

Sir Oliver said:

"I'll plague you every way."

He drank the almond milk and said:

"Look, do you see? It is gone."

"May a pox go with it," Lady Kix said.

"Aye, curse and don't spare words now," Sir Oliver said.

"Stir up and down, sir," Touchwood Senior said. "You must not stand still."

This was part of the treatment: exercise (riding on horseback, dancing, and leaping) in addition to a nutritious diet.

"Nay, I'm not given to standing," Sir Oliver said.

He was not given to having erections.

Touchwood Senior began, "So much the better, sir, for the —"

Sir Oliver said:

"I never yet could stand long in one place. I learned it from my father, who was always fidgety.

"What if I crossed this, sir?"

He danced, including some steps or jumps with crossed legs.

The movements were intended to help the almond milk to work.

Touchwood Senior said:

"O, that is surpassingly good, sir, and it would show well on horseback."

If Sir Oliver were to ride on horseback with crossed legs, he would be riding side-saddle, like a woman.

Touchwood Senior continued:

"When you come to your inn, if you leapt over a joint-stool or two, it would be not amiss —"

He said to himself:

"— although you broke your neck, sir."

One meaning of "leap" is "have sex."

"What do you say to a table thus high, sir?" Sir Oliver asked, pointing to a table.

Touchwood Senior said:

"Nothing is better, sir —"

He added to himself, "— if it is furnished with good victuals — good food."

He then asked:

"You remember how the bargain runs about this business?"

Continuing to dance, Sir Oliver said:

"Or else I had a bad head."

He meant that if he had forgotten that, his head would be bad, but soon, his head would bear the invisible horns of a cuckold.

Sir Oliver continued:

"You must receive, sir, four hundred pounds from me in four separate payments. One hundred pounds now in hand."

"Right, that I have, sir," Touchwood Senior said.

Sir Oliver said:

"Another hundred when my wife is quick: when she is pregnant, and the fetus is kicking.

"The third when she's brought to bed, and the last hundred when the child cries; for if it should be stillborn, it does no good, sir."

Touchwood Senior said:

"All this is even still — it is still in effect."

He then said:

"A little faster, sir."

"Not a whit, sir, I'm in an excellent pace for any medicine," Sir Oliver said.

A servant entered and said, "Your white mare's ready."

Sir Oliver said to the servant:

"I shall go up immediately."

If the medicine worked, his penis would go up, too.

He then said to his wife:

"One kiss, and farewell."

"Thou shall have two, love," Lady Kix said.

They kissed. Twice.

"Expect me about three o'clock," Sir Oliver said.

"With all my heart, sweet," Lady Kix said.

Sir Oliver exited.

Touchwood Senior said to himself:

"By this light, they have forgotten their anger they had previously, and they are as far in love again as ever they were. Which way the devil did they come to make up? By God's heart, I didn't see them. Their ways are beyond finding out."

He was wondering how they had come to this point of being lovey-dovey again.

He then said to Lady Kix:

"Come, sweet lady."

"How must I take my medicine, sir?" Lady Kix asked.

"Clean contrary to how your husband takes his medicine," Touchwood Senior said. "Your medicine must be taken lying down."

"Clean contrary" means "completely differently": 1) lying down, not standing up, and 2) not by mouth, but in a different opening.

Lady Kix asked, "In bed, sir?"

"In bed, or wherever you prefer for your own ease," Touchwood Senior said. "Your coach will serve."

In this society, many affairs were conducted in coaches.

"The medicine must necessarily please," Lady Kix said.

They exited.

CHAPTER 4

— 4.1 —

Tim and his tutor talked together in Yellowhammer's house.

"*Negatur argumentum*, tutor," Tim said.

["Your argument is denied, tutor."]

"*Probo tibi, pupil, stultus non est animal rationale*," his tutor said.

["I am proving to you, pupil, that a fool is not a rational animal."]

"*Falleris sane*," Tim said.

["Indeed, you will fail."]

"*Quaeso ut taceas. Probo tibi*," his tutor said.

["I ask that you be quiet. I am proving it to you."]

"*Quomodo probas, domine?*" Tim said.

["How will you prove it, teacher?"]

"*Stultus non habet rationem; ergo, non est animal rationale*," his tutor said.

["A fool has no reason; therefore, he is not a rational animal."]

"*Sic argumentaris, domine: Stultus non habet rationem, ergo non est animal rationale. Negatur argumentum* again, tutor," Tim said.

["So you are arguing, teacher: A fool has no reason; therefore, he is not a rational animal. Your argument is denied again, tutor."]

"*Argumentum iterum probo tibi, domine: Qui non participat de ratione nullo modo potest vocari rationalibus*, but *stultus non participat de ratione, ergo stultus nullo modo potest dicere rationali*," his tutor said.

["I will prove the thesis again to you: He who does not participate in reason can in no way be called rational, but a fool does not participate in reason; therefore, a fool can in no way be said to be rational."]

In other words:

Premise 1: A man who does not participate in reason is not a rational animal.

Premise 2: A fool does not participate in reason.

Conclusion: A fool is not a rational animal.

"*Participat*," Tim said.

["He (a fool) does participate (in reason)."]

"*Sic disputus. Qui participat quomodo participate?*" his tutor asked.

["So you say. How does the participater participate?"]

"*Ut homo. Probabo tibi in syllogismo,*" Tim said.

["As a man. I will prove it to you in a syllogism."]

"*Hunc proba,*" his tutor said.

["Prove it."]

"*Sic probo, domine: Stultus est homo sicut tu et ego sum; homo est animal rationale, sicut stultus est animal rationale,*" Tim said.

["I prove it thus, teacher: A fool is a man just as you are and I am; a man is a rational animal, so a fool is a rational animal."]

In other words:

Premise 1: A fool is a man.

Premise 2: Men are rational animals.

Conclusion: A fool is a rational animal.

According to Tim, a fool is a man just as Tim are and his tutor are. Therefore, according to Tim, he and his tutor are fools.

Maudlin entered the scene.

"Here's nothing but disputing — arguing — all day long with them," she said.

The tutor said to Tim, "*Sic disputus: Stultus est homo sicut tu et ego sum; homo est animal rationale, sicut stultus est animal rationale.*"

["You argue thus: A fool is a man just as you and I are; a man is a rational animal, so a fool is a rational animal."]

Maudlin said:

"Your reasons are both good, whatever they are."

Tim's tutor was arguing that Humankind is a rational animal, which means that human beings are as a species capable of reason. This does not necessarily mean that each human being is capable of reason.

Tim was arguing that each human being individually is capable of reason and therefore since a fool is a human being, then the fool is capable of reason.

Tim's argument is bad because it has a false premise. It is false that every human being is capable of reason.

By the way, one argument for women's rights is that the world needs good brains, and if the world doesn't use women's brains, then it isn't using half the good brains in the world.

Maudlin continued:

"Please give them over. Truly, you'll tire yourselves. What's the matter between you? What issue are you discussing?"

"Nothing but reasoning about a fool, mother," Tim said.

"About a fool, son?" Maudlin asked. "Alas, why do you need to trouble your heads about that; none of us all but knows what a fool is."

In other words: Everyone knows what a fool is.

"Why, what's a fool, mother?" Tim said. "I come to you now."

His last sentence means: I pose the question to you. Answer it.

"Why, a fool is one who is married before he has wit," Maudlin said.

"It is pretty, indeed, and well guessed of a woman who was never brought up at the university," Tim said, "but bring forth what fool you will, mother, I'll prove him to be as reasonable a creature as myself or my tutor here."

One way for Maudlin to bring forth a fool is to give birth to one.

Tim would now prove — demonstrate — that he is as reasonable a creature as a fool.

"Ha! It is impossible," Maudlin said.

"Nay, he shall do it, indeed," Tim's tutor said.

"It is the easiest thing to prove a fool by logic," Tim said. "By logic I'll prove anything."

With contradictory premises, you can prove anything.

Premise 1: A.

Premise 2: Not A.

Premise 3: A or Anything.

Conclusion: Anything (from P2 and P3).

For example:

Premise 1: Two plus two equals four.

Premise 2: Two plus two does not equal four.

Premise 3: Either two plus two equals four or Anything.

Conclusion: Anything (from P2 and P3)

"Anything" is any statement at all.

For example: David Bruce is a better writer than William Shakespeare.

Of course, a good argument will have all true and no false premises.

It is up to the reader to decide whether "David Bruce is a better writer than William Shakespeare" would be a true or a false premise. /s

"What! Thou will not!" Maudlin said.

"I'll prove a whore to be an honest woman," Tim said.

Cough. (Foreshadowing.) Cough.

"Nay, by my faith, she must prove that herself, or logic will never do it," Maudlin said.

"Logic will do it, I tell you," Tim said.

"Some in this street would give a thousand pounds if you could prove their wives so," Maudlin said.

Tim said:

"Indeed, I can, and all their daughters, too, even if each daughter had three bastards."

He then asked:

"When does your tailor come here?"

A stereotype of tailors was that they are lecherous. Another was that they lacked courage.

A proverb stated, "Nine tailors make but one man."

"Why, what about him?" Maudlin asked.

"By logic I'll prove him to be a man," Tim said. "Let him come when he will."

Tim's second sentence has a bawdy meaning.

"How hard at first was learning to him!" Maudlin said to Tim's tutor. "Truly, sir, I thought he would never have taken the Latin tongue. How many accidences do you think he wore out before he came to his grammar?"

An "accidence" is a book giving the rules for forming the ends of Latin words. "Accidents" are "inflections."

Grammars are more complex than accidences because grammars give information about forming Latin sentences.

"Some three or four," Tim's tutor said.

"Believe me, sir, some four and thirty," Maudlin said.

"Pish, I made haberdines of them in church porches," Tim said.

A haberdine is a dried codfish. Children played a game using paper fish. Tim tore up his schoolbooks so he could cut the pages into paper fish.

"Cod" can also mean "scrotum."

A church "porch" can be a church's "side chapel."

"He was eight years in his grammar," Maudlin said, "and stuck horribly at a foolish place there called *as in presenti*."

As in presenti is a phrase that appears in a Latin grammar book: Lyly and Colet's *A Short Introduction to Grammar*.

Some Latin words end in *-as*.

"Pox, I have it here now," Tim said.

He had that grammar book with him — it was probably among the books he had brought with him from Cambridge.

He also had an *ass in* his *presence*.

"He so shamed me once before an honest gentleman who knew me when I was a maiden," Maudlin said.

The gentleman may have known her Biblically.

"These women must have all out," Tim said. "They must tell everything."

Tim's mother was exposing Tim to ridicule by telling tales about him.

Maudlin said, "*Quid est grammatica?* [What is grammar?] says the gentleman to Tim — I shall remember by a sweet, sweet token — but nothing could Tim answer."

Tim's tutor answered, "How about now, pupil? Ha! *Quid est grammatica?*"

Tim said:

"*Grammatica?*"

He laughed:

"Ha! Ha! Ha!"

Both Tim's tutor and Tim were amused because the standard answer to the question used the word *ars*, which made sniggering schoolboys immediately think of the word "arse."

Maudlin said, "Nay, do not laugh, son, but let me hear you say it now. There was one word that went so prettily off the gentleman's tongue that I shall remember it the longest day of my life — that is, as long as I live."

Tim's tutor again asked Tim, "Come, *quid est grammatica?*"

Tim said, "Are you not ashamed, tutor? *Grammatica?* Why, *recte scribendi atque loquendi ars*, sir-reverence of my mother."

["Why, the art of writing and speaking correctly."]

"Sir-reverence" means 1) begging the pardon, and 2) excrement.

Tim may have been apologizing to his mother for his saying *ars*, which is close to "arse."

Maudlin said:

"That was it, indeed. That was the token."

She meant the word *ars*.

Maudlin continued:

"Why, now, son, I see you are a deep scholar; and master tutor, let me have a word with you, please.

"Let us withdraw a little into my husband's chamber. I'll send in the North Wales gentlewoman to him to keep him company; she expects to be wooed. I'll put together both, and I'll lock the door."

Maudlin's husband's chamber can also be Maudlin's vagina.

"Put together both" can mean 1) put Tim and the Welsh gentlewoman together, and/or 2) put Maudlin's vagina and Tim's tutor's penis together.

Maudlin and the tutor might have been about to make Maudlin's husband a cuckold.

"I give great approbation to your conclusion," Tim's tutor said.

Maudlin and Tim's tutor exited, perhaps to have sex.

Alone, Tim said to himself:

"I marvel who this gentlewoman should be whom I should have in marriage; she's a stranger to me. I wonder what my parents mean, indeed, to match me with a stranger so."

Tim's parents wanted him to marry the Welsh gentlewoman.

Tim continued:

"She's a maiden who is neither kiff [kith] nor kin to me."

"Kith" means "friends and acquaintances."

Tim continued:

"By God's life, do they think I have no more concern for my body than to lie with someone whom I never knew, a complete stranger, one who never went to school with me neither, nor were we ever playfellows together.

"They're mightily overseen — mistaken — in it, I think.

"They say she has mountains as the dowry to her marriage. She's full of cattle, some two thousand runts. Now what the meaning of these runts should be, my tutor cannot tell me.

"I have looked in *Rider's Dictionary* for the letter R, and there I can hear no tidings of these runts neither. Unless they are Rumford hogs, I don't know what they are."

"Runts" are a breed of small Welsh cattle.

The town of Rumford had a hog market.

John Rider wrote a Latin/English, English/Latin dictionary. The word "runt" is not defined in it.

The Welsh gentlewoman entered the scene.

Seeing her, Tim said to himself:

"And here she comes.

"If I know what to say to her now in the way of marriage, I'm no graduate."

Tim was a graduate, and he did not know what to say to her about marriage.

Tim continued saying to himself:

"I think, indeed, it is boldly done of her to come into my chamber since she is only a stranger.

"She shall not say I'm so proud yet, but I'll speak to her."

He did not want her to be able to say that he was haughty and arrogant, and so he would speak to her.

Tim continued saying to himself:

By the Virgin Mary, as I will order it, she shall 'take no hold of my words, I'll warrant — guarantee — her."

Time thought that the Welsh gentlewoman would be unable to mistake — misunderstand — his words. Instead, she will be unable to take — understand — his words.

The Welsh gentlewoman looked at him and curtsied to him.

Tim continued saying to himself:

"She looks and makes a curtsey."

Tim said to her:

"*Salve tu quoque puella pulcherrima, quid vis nescio nec sane curo.*"

["Hello to you, also, most beautiful girl. What you want, I don't know nor do I care."]

Tim then said to himself:

"Tully's own phrase to a heart."

Tully is Marcus Tullius Cicero. He did not write those Latin words.

"To a heart" means "to perfection."

The Welsh gentlewoman, who did not know Latin, said to herself, "I don't know what he means; a suitor, he said? I bet my life that he understands no English."

Tim then said to her, "*Ferter* [pronounced 'farter'] *me hercule tu virgo, wallia ut opibus abundis maximis.*"

["It has been said to me by Hercules, young woman, that Wales abounds with the greatest wealth."]

Or: ["It has been said to me by Hercules, young woman, that you abound with the greatest wealth in Wales."]

The Welsh gentlewoman said to herself, "What's this *ferter* and *abundundis*? He mocks me, to be sure, and he calls me a bundle of farts."

Tim said to himself:

"I have no Latin word now for their runts; I'll make some shift — some contrivance — or other.

He then said to the Welsh gentlewoman:

"*Iterum, dico opibus abundat maximis montibus et fontibus et, ut ita dicam, rontibus; attamen, vero, homanculus ego sum natura, simule arte bachalarius, lecto profecto non parata.*"

Tim's "shift" was to invent the "Latin" word *rontibus*, meaning "with runts."

["Again, I say that it (it = Wales, or your wealth) is abundant with the greatest mountains and fountains and, as I say thus, with runts; however, truly, I am a little man by nature and a bachelor by art, truly not prepared for bed."]

Tim was "*lecto profecto non parata*": "truly not prepared for bed."

Parata is in the feminine case, although Tim had used the word to refer to himself.

The Welsh gentlewoman said to herself:

"This is very strange; maybe he can speak Welsh."

She then said to Tim:

"*Avedera whee comrage? Derdue cog foginis?*"

["Can you speak Welsh? For God's sake, are you mocking me?"]

Tim said to himself, "*Cog foggin*? I scorn to cog with her, I'll tell her so, too, in a word near her own language."

He said to her:

"*Ego non cogo.*"

["I will not get together (with you)" or "I will not force (you)."]

The English word "cog" means "cheat," so presumably Tim was trying to say, "I will not cheat."

The Welsh gentlewoman said to him, "*Rhegosin a whiggin harle ron corid ambre.*"

["Some cheese and after talking a walk."]

A stereotype of the Welsh people was that Welsh people loved cheese.

Tim said to himself:

"By my faith, she's a good scholar, I see that already. She has the tongues — languages — plain."

Readers will soon learn that Tim thought that the Welsh gentlewoman had been speaking Hebrew to him.

Tim continued saying to himself:

"I bet my life that she has travelled. What will folks say? 'There goes the learned couple.' Indeed, if the truth were known, she has proceeded."

"Proceeded" can mean 1) graduated, and 2) proceeded past virginity.

At this time, women could not study at or get degrees from Cambridge: a waste of female brains.

Maudlin entered the scene.

"How are things now?" Maudlin asked. "How speeds your business? Are you successful?"

"I'm glad my mother's come to part us," Tim said to himself.

Maudlin asked the Welsh gentlewoman, "How do you agree, indeed? How are you getting along?"

"As well as ever we did before we met," the Welsh gentlewoman said.

"How's that?" Maudlin asked.

"You put me together with a man I don't understand," the Welsh gentlewoman said. "Your son's no English man, I think."

"No English man, bless my boy, and born in the heart of London?" Maudlin asked.

"I have been long enough in the chamber with him," the Welsh gentlewoman said, "and I find neither Welsh nor English in him."

"Why, Tim, how have you used — treated — the gentlewoman?" Maudlin asked.

"As well as a man might do, mother, in modest Latin," Tim answered.

"Latin, fool?" Maudlin said.

"And she recoiled in Hebrew," Tim said.

By "recoiled," Tim meant "replied."

"In Hebrew, fool?" Maudlin said. "It is Welsh."

"All comes to one, mother," Tim said.

In other words: Welsh? Hebrew? They are basically the same.

"She can speak English, too," Maudlin said.

"Who told me so much?" Tim said. "By God's heart, if she can speak English, I'll clap to her. I thought you'd marry me to a stranger."

Since the Welsh gentlewoman could speak English, he was willing to marry her. He would also applaud her.

Maudlin said to the Welsh gentlewoman, "You must forgive him. He's so inured to Latin, he and his tutor, that he has quite forgotten to use the Protestant tongue."

Latin was the language of the Mass, and so Latin was the Catholic tongue.

In Great Britain, Protestant religious services were held in English, and so English was the Protestant tongue, aka language.

"It is quickly pardoned, indeed," the Welsh gentlewoman said.

Maudlin said:

"Tim, make amends and kiss her."

She then said to the Welsh gentlewoman:

"He makes towards you, indeed."

Tim kissed the Welsh gentlewoman.

He then said:

"O, delicious, one may discover her country by her kissing. It is a true saying that there's nothing tastes so sweet as your Welsh mutton."

"Country" was a word commonly used to pun on "cunt."

"Mutton" was slang for "whore."

Tim then said to her:

"It was reported you could sing."

"Sing" can also mean "have sex."

Maudlin said, "O, she sings splendidly, Tim, the sweetest British songs."

"And it is my mind, I swear, that before I marry that I would see all my wife's good parts at once, to view how rich I were," Tim said.

"Parts" can mean 1) accomplishments, or 2) private parts.

Maudlin said:

"Thou shall hear sweet music, Tim."

She then said to the Welsh gentlewoman:

"Please, truly."

The Welsh gentlewoman sang:

"*Cupid is Venus' only joy,*

"*But he is a wanton boy,*

"*A very, very wanton boy,*

"*He shoots at ladies' naked breasts,*

"*He is the cause of most men's crests,*"

The "crests" are the horns of a cuckold.

The Welsh gentlewoman continued to sing:

"*I mean upon the forehead,*

"*Invisible but horrid;*

"*It was he first taught upon the way*

"*To keep a lady's lips in play.*"

The word "lips" can mean *labia majora* and *labia minora*.

The Welsh gentlewoman continued to sing:

"*Why should not Venus chide her son,*

"*For the pranks that he has done,*

"*The wanton pranks that he has done?*

"*He shoots his fiery darts so thick,*"

The fiery darts that are shot may be streams of semen from a penis.

The Welsh gentlewoman continued to sing:

"*They hurt poor ladies to the quick,*"

The "quick" is the tenderest, most sensitive part. Also, when a woman is quick, she is pregnant.

The Welsh gentlewoman continued to sing:

"*Ah me, with cruel wounding;*

"*His darts are so confounding,*

"*That life and sense would soon decay,*

"*But [Except] that he keeps their lips in play.*

"*Can there be any part of bliss,*

"*In a quickly fleeting kiss,*

"*A quickly fleeting kiss?*

"*To one's pleasure, leisures are but waste,*"

"*The slowest kiss makes too much haste,*"

In other words: When it comes to seeking pleasure, one ought not to be slothful, but although we want sexual pleasure immediately, we also want it to last.

A line rhyming with "find it" may be missing below.

The Welsh gentlewoman continued to sing:

"*And lose it ere [before] we find it,*

"*The pleasing sport they only know,*

"*That close above and close below.*"

The "pleasing sport" involved lips above and below.

"I would not change my wife for a kingdom," Tim said. "I can do somewhat, too, in my own lodging."

The word "do" can mean "have sex." Tim was probably talking about masturbation.

And he also probably would not exchange his (future) wife for a kingdom.

Yellowhammer and Allwit entered the scene. Allwit was in disguise, and Yellowhammer did not know who he was.

Yellowhammer said to Tim:

"Why, well said, Tim, the bells go merrily. I love such peals of marriage bells, as I love life.

"Wife, lead them inside for a while. Here's a strange gentleman who desires a private conference with me.

Maudlin, Tim, and the Welsh gentlewoman exited.

Yellowhammer then said to the disguised Allwit, who was using the name "Yellowhammer" and who was pretending to be a distant relative of Yellowhammer's:

"You're welcome, sir, the more for your name's sake. Good Master Yellowhammer, I love my name well, and which of the Yellowhammers take you descent from, if I may be so bold with you. Which, I ask?"

"The Yellowhammers in Oxfordshire, near Abbington," the disguised Allwit said.

Yellowhammer said:

"And those are the best Yellowhammers, and the truest bred. I came from there myself, although I am now a citizen."

He was a citizen in the sense that he was a freeman in the goldsmiths' guild of London.

Yellowhammer continued:

"I'll be bold with you; you are most welcome."

"I hope the zeal I bring with me shall deserve it," the disguised Allwit said.

"I hope no less," Yellowhammer said. "What is your will, sir? What do you want, sir?"

"I understand by rumors that you have a daughter, which my bold love shall henceforth title 'cousin,'" the disguised Allwit said.

The word "cousin" meant "kin."

"I thank you for her, sir," Yellowhammer said.

"I have heard of her virtues and other confirmed and established graces," the disguised Allwit said.

"She is a plaguy and troublesome girl, sir," Yellowhammer said.

"Her reputation sets her out with richer ornaments than you are pleased to boast of. It is done modestly," the disguised Allwit said. "I hear she's thinking about marriage."

"You hear the truth, sir," Yellowhammer said.

"And with a knight in town, Sir Walter Whorehound," the disguised Allwit said.

"The very same, sir," Yellowhammer said.

"I am the sorrier for it," the disguised Allwit said.

"The sorrier? Why, cousin?" Yellowhammer asked.

"It is not too far past, is it?" the disguised Allwit asked. "It may be yet recalled and rescinded?"

"Recalled and rescinded?" Yellowhammer asked. "Why, good sir?"

"If you can satisfy me on that single point, you shall hear why from me," the disguised Allwit said.

"There's no legal marriage contract passed," Yellowhammer said.

"I am very joyful, sir," the disguised Allwit said.

"But he's the man who must bed her," Yellowhammer said.

The disguised Allwit said:

"By no means, coz. She's quite undone and ruined then, and you'll curse the time that you ever made the match."

"Coz" means "cousin."

The disguised Allwit continued:

"Sir Walter is an arrant and complete whoremaster, which consumes his time and state — he to my knowledge has kept this seven years, coz, another man's wife, too."

"O, abominable!" Yellowhammer said.

The disguised Allwit said, "He maintains the whole house, apparels the husband, pays servants' wages, not so much, but —"

Yellowhammer interrupted, "— worse and worse, and does the husband know this?"

"Know?" the disguised Allwit said. "Aye, and he is glad he may, too: It is his living as other trades thrive, butchers by selling flesh, poulters by venting conies, or the like, coz."

Poulters 1) sell poultry, or 2) sell women. "Poulters" can mean "bawds."

"Venting conies" can mean 1) selling rabbits, or 2) selling women.

Allwit sells his wife.

"What an incomparable wittol is this man!" Yellowhammer said.

"Tush, he cares no more about that, believe me, coz, than I do," the disguised Allwit said.

"What a base slave is that man!" Yellowhammer said.

"All's one to him," the disguised Allwit said. "He doesn't care. He feeds and takes his ease; he was never yet the man who ever broke his sleep to beget a child by his own confession, and yet his wife has seven children."

"What! By Sir Walter?" Yellowhammer asked.

"Sir Walter's likely to keep — to support — them, and to maintain them, in excellent fashion," the disguised Allwit said. "He dares do no less, sir."

"By God's life, has he children, too?" Yellowhammer asked.

He wanted confirmation that Sir Walter Whorehound had fathered the children with Mistress Allwit.

"Children?" the disguised Allwit said. "He has boys thus high" — he held up his hand — "in their Cato and Cordelius."

Dionysius Cato wrote *Disticha de Moribus* [*Couplets on Morals*].

Maturini Corderii [Mathurin Cordier] wrote *Colloquia Scholastica* [*Scholastic Conversations*].

These were famous textbooks of the time.

"What! You jest, sir!" Yellowhammer said.

"Why, one can write a Latin verse and is now at Eton College," the disguised Allwit said.

"O, this news has cut into my heart, coz," Yellowhammer said.

"It had eaten nearer and deeper if it had not been anticipated and prevented," the disguised Allwit said. "The mother is one Allwit's wife."

"Allwit?" Yellowhammer said. "By God's foot, I have heard of him. Didn't he have a girl kursened — that is, christened — recently?"

"Aye, that work did cost the knight — Sir Walter — more than a hundred marks," the disguised Allwit said.

"I'll mark him for a knave and a villain for it," Yellowhammer said. "A thousand thanks and blessings. I have done with him."

The disguised Allwit said to himself:

"Ha! Ha! Ha! This knight — Sir Walter — will stick by my ribs still. He will stick with me. I shall not lose him yet."

According to Allwit, Sir Walter would also stick by his — Allwit's — rib, aka wife.

The disguised Allwit continued saying to himself:

"No legal wife will come to him; he will not marry. Wherever he woos, I find him still at home! Ha! Ha!"

The disguised Allwit exited.

Alone, Yellowhammer said to himself what he really thought:

"Well, let's grant all this. Let's say now that his deeds are black. Well, what serves marriage, but to call him back and reform him.

"I have kept a whore myself, and had a bastard, by Mistress Anne, *in Anno* —."

In anno is Latin for "in the year." It is also a pun on "in Anne — O!"

Possibly, Yellowhammer does not want to remember the year, if it would reveal him to be old.

You, the reader, may fill in a suitable year. If the year is in the early 1600s, Yellowhammer and the bastard would be quite old now.

Yellowhammer continued saying to himself:

"I don't care who knows I have a bastard; he's now a jolly fellow. He has been twice warden, and so may Sir Walter's fruit — his children — be. They were but basely begotten, and so was my bastard son."

Yellowhammer's bastard was either a churchwarden or a member of one of the City companies' governing bodies.

A "warden" is also a species of pear. Bastards are forbidden fruit: illegitimate children.

Yellowhammer continued saying to himself:

"The knight is rich, and he shall be my son-in-law. His keeping a whore doesn't matter as long as the whore he keeps is wholesome and healthy. My daughter takes no hurt then, so let them wed. I'll have him sweat well before they go to bed."

Sweating was a treatment for venereal disease.

Maudlin entered the scene and said, "O husband, husband!"

"How are things now, Maudlin?" Yellowhammer asked.

"We are all undone and ruined!" Maudlin said. "She's gone! She's gone!"

"Again?" Yellowhammer said. "By God's death, which way?"

Maudlin said:

"Over the houses' roofs.

"Lay — search — the waterside! Or else she's gone forever!"

Yellowhammer said, "O venturous — bold — baggage!"

Yellowhammer and Maudlin exited.

Tim and his tutor talked together.

"Thieves, thieves, my sister's stolen — some thief has got her," Tim said. "O, how miraculously did my father's plate escape. It was all left out, tutor."

"Is it possible?" Tim's tutor asked.

Tim said:

"Besides, three chains — necklaces — of pearl and a box of coral were left out.

"My sister's gone. Let's look at Trig stairs for her. My mother's gone to lay — search — the Common stairs at Puddle wharf, and at the dock below stands my poor silly — pitiable — father."

Trig stairs and the Common stairs were places where passengers could embark on boats.

"Run, sweet tutor, run."

Tim and his tutor exited.

On a bank of the Thames, both the Touchwoods — Senior and Junior — talked together.

Touchwood Senior said:

"I would have been taken and arrested, brother, by eight sheriff's sergeants, if not for the honest watermen. I am bound to them. They are the most requiteful people living, for as they get their means — that is, earn their living — by gentlemen, they are always the most eager to help gentlemen."

The watermen were men who ferried passengers in small boats across the Thames River.

"Requiteful" means "willing to return favors."

Touchwood Senior continued:

"You heard how one escaped out of the Blackfriars Theater just a while since from two or three varlets who came into the house with all their rapiers drawn, as if they'd dance the sword dance on the stage, with candles in their hands like chandlers' ghosts, while the poor gentleman who was so pursued and bandied and buffeted was safely landed by an honest pair of oars."

Chandlers are candle-makers.

Stage ghosts carried distinctive items.

The ruffians perhaps needed candles to see well in the theater. Or perhaps they were pretending to be stage ghosts.

"I love them with my heart for it," Touchwood Junior said.

Four watermen entered the scene.

"Your first man, sir," the first waterman said.

The waterman's cry meant "My boat is the first in line."

"Shall I carry you gentlemen with a pair of oars?" the second waterman asked.

"These are the honest fellows," Touchwood Senior said. "Take one pair of oars and leave the rest of the oars for her."

"Her" was Moll, who was supposed to be coming soon.

"Barn Elms," Touchwood Junior said.

Barn Elms was a manor-house and park upstream.

"You need say no more, brother," Touchwood Senior said.

"Your first man," the first waterman said again.

"Shall I carry your worship?" the second waterman asked.

Touchwood Junior said to Touchwood Senior and the first and second watermen:

"Go."

Touchwood Senior and the first and second watermen exited.

Touchwood Junior would depart from another place.

Touchwood Junior then said:

"And you honest watermen who stay, here's a French crown for you."

He gave them a French crown.

A French crown is a coin.

Then he said:

"A maiden is coming with all speed to take water. Row her lustily — that is, vigorously — to Barn Elms after me."

"To take water" means 1) to embark, and 2) to be a receptacle for semen.

"To Barn Elms, good sir," the third waterman said. "Make ready the boat, Sam. We'll wait below."

Moll was late in coming, so Touchwood Junior was going to leave by another wharf. He had arranged transportation so that Moll could follow him.

The third waterman and Sam (the fourth and final waterman) exited.

Moll entered the scene.

"What made you stay — take — so long?" Touchwood Junior asked.

"I found the way more dangerous than I looked for," Moll answered.

"Leave quickly, there's a boat that waits for you, and I'll take water at Paul's wharf, and overtake you," Touchwood Junior said.

Moll would now embark first, and Touchwood Junior would pay his waterman or watermen more to row fast and overtake her.

"Good sir, do, we cannot be too safe," Moll said.

The boats must have been small if they could carry only one passenger.

They exited.

Sir Walter Whorehound, Yellowhammer, Tim, and Tim's tutor were searching for Moll.

"By God's life, do you call this close keeping?" Sir Walter Whorehound complained.

Yellowhammer had been close keeping Moll; that is, he had been keeping her locked up at home.

"She was kept under a double lock," Yellowhammer said.

"A double devil," Sir Walter said.

"That's a buff sergeant, tutor," Tim said about Sir Walter. "He'll never wear out."

"Buff" was a kind of ox-hide leather worn by sergeants, who could make arrests and often were dogged in doing their duty.

"How would you have women locked?" Yellowhammer asked.

"With padlocks, father — the Venetians are accustomed to do it," Tim said. "My tutor reads it."

Padlocks were used on doors and on chastity belts.

"Reads" can mean "advises," but the tutor probably has read about this practice.

"By God's heart, if she were so locked up, how did she get out?" Sir Walter asked.

"There was a little hole that looked — that opened — into the roof gutter, but who would have dreamt of that?" Yellowhammer said.

"A wiser man would," Sir Walter said.

"He says the truth, father," Tim said. "A wise man for love will seek every hole. My tutor knows it."

"Every hole." Say no more.

Tim's tutor said, "*Verum poeta dicit.*"

["The poet says the truth."]

"*Dicit Virgilius*, father," Tim said.

["Virgil says, father."]

The lascivious Ovid, who wrote a seduction manual, was much more likely than the highly moral Virgil to say, "A wise man for love will seek every hole."

Ovid's *Ars Amatoria*, Book 2, lines 243-246 states:

Picking up on the name "Virgil," Yellowhammer said:

"Please, talk of thy jills somewhere else; she's played the jill with me."

"Jills" are "wenches."

He then asked:

"Where's your wise mother now?"

"Run mad, I think," Tim said. "I thought she would have drowned herself. She would not stay and wait for oars but took a smelt boat. Surely, I think she has gone fishing for her."

Smelt are small fish. Smelt are also fools.

"She'll catch a goodly dish of gudgeons now that will serve us all for supper," Yellowhammer said.

In other words: She will make all of us look like fools.

Like smelt, gudgeons are small fish. They are also fools.

Maudlin entered the scene, drawing Moll by the hair. Moll was dripping wet. Some watermen came with them.

"I'll tug thee home by the hair," Maudlin said.

"Good mistress, spare her," the watermen said.

"Tend — mind — your own business," Maudlin said.

"You are a cruel mother," the watermen said.

Then they exited.

"O, my heart dies!" Moll said.

"I'll make thee an example for all the neighbors' daughters," Maudlin said.

"Farewell, life," Moll said.

"You who have tricks can counterfeit tears," Maudlin said.

"Hold back, hold back, Maudlin," Yellowhammer said.

"I have brought your jewel by the hair," Maudlin said.

"She's here, knight," Yellowhammer said to Sir Walter.

Sir Walter said to Yellowhammer and Maudlin, "Forbear or I'll grow worse — I'll grow angrier."

"Look at her, tutor," Tim said. "My mother has brought her from the water like a mermaid; she's only half my sister now. She's my sister as far as the flesh goes; the rest may be sold to fishwives."

Mermaids are part flesh and part fish.

"Mermaid" is a cant word for "whore," and "fishmonger" is a cant word for "bawd."

Fishwives and fishmongers sell fish.

"Dissembling, cunning baggage!" Maudlin said.

"Impudent strumpet!" Yellowhammer said.

Sir Walter said to Yellowhammer and Maudlin:

"Either give over both, or I'll give over."

In other words: Stop yelling at her, or I'll decline to marry her.

Sir Walter then said to Moll:

"Why have you treated me like this, unkind mistress? Wherein have I deserved to be treated like this?"

Yellowhammer said to Sir Walter:

"You talk too fondly and foolishly, sir.

"We'll take another course and prevent all. We might have done it long ago; we'll lose no time now, nor trust to it any longer.

"Tomorrow morning, as early as sunrise, we'll have you joined in matrimony."

"O, bring me death tonight, love-pitying Fates," Moll said. "Don't let me see tomorrow in the living world."

The three Fates commanded the pulse of life; they controlled human life. Clotho spun the thread of life. Lachesis measured the thread of life, determining how long a person lived. Atropos cut the thread of life; when the thread was cut, the person died.

"Are you content, sir, that until then — until the wedding — she shall be watched?" Yellowhammer asked Sir Walter.

"Baggage, you shall be watched," Maudlin said to Moll.

Maudlin, Moll, and Yellowhammer exited.

"Why, father, my tutor and I will both watch in armor," Tim said as his father exited.

One meaning of "in armor" is "made bold by drinking alcoholic beverages."

"What shall we do for weapons?" Tim's tutor asked.

"Don't worry about that," Tim said. "If need be, I can send for conquering metal, tutor, that never lost day yet. It is just at Westminster Abbey. I am acquainted with the man who keeps the Monuments there. I can borrow Harry the Fifth's sword; it will serve us both to watch with."

Actually, King Henry V's sword and armor had been stolen.

Tim was probably thinking of King Edward III's double-handed sword, which was seven feet long.

Tim and his tutor exited.

Alone, Sir Walter said to himself, "I never was so near my wish as this chance makes me. Before tomorrow noon, I shall receive two thousand pounds in gold, and a sweet maidenhead worth forty pounds."

The two thousand pounds in gold were the dowry.

Virgins could be sold. The defloration of a virgin was expensive.

Touchwood Junior and a waterman entered the scene.

"O, thy news metaphorically splits me and causes me to shipwreck," Touchwood Junior said.

"Half drowned, she was cruelly tugged by the hair, and her mother, unlike a mother, forced her disgracefully," the waterman said.

Touchwood Junior said:

"Enough, leave me like my joys."

The waterman exited.

Touchwood Junior then said to Sir Walter:

"Sir, haven't you seen a wretched maiden pass this way?

"By God's heart, villain, is it thou?"

"Yes, slave, it is I," Sir Walter said.

The two men drew their swords.

"I must break through thee then," Touchwood Junior said. "There is no stop that checks my tongue and keeps me from speaking and wooing and that checks all my hopeful fortunes, that breast of yours excepted, and I must have way."

A dog following a scent "gives tongue" and howls.

Touchwood Junior was following the scent of Moll so he could find and marry her.

"Sir, I believe it will hold your life in play — that is, at risk," Sir Walter said.

The phrase "in play" is from a card game.

Many duels ended with a death.

The two men fought, and Sir Walter wounded Touchwood Junior.

"Sir, you'll think you'll gain — wound — the heart in my breast at the first thrust?" Touchwood Junior asked.

"There is no making a deal with you then?" Sir Walter said. "Think about the dowry for two thousand pounds."

Either Sir Walter wanted to bribe Touchwood Junior to not fight him and to give up Moll, or he knew that he could not make a deal with him and so he was thinking about the dowry to stiffen his resolve to fight.

Not everyone wants to fight a duel, even if they drew first blood.

Sir Walter had much money coming to him if he lived. He would lose that money if he died.

The two men fought, and Touchwood Junior wounded Sir Walter.

"O, now my wound is requited, sir," Touchwood Junior said.

"And being of even hand, I'll play no longer," Sir Walter said.

Both men were wounded. They were even.

"No longer, slave?" Touchwood Junior asked.

"I have certain things to think about, before I dare go further," Sir Walter said.

Being wounded can make one think about death and what awaits one after death.

Touchwood Junior said:

"Just one bout?

"I'll follow thee to death, but I'll have it out."

They exited.

CHAPTER 5

— 5.1 —

Allwit, his wife, and Davy Dahumma talked together.

"This is a misery of a house," Mistress Allwit said.

"What shall become of us?" Allwit asked.

"I think his wound is mortal," Davy said about Sir Walter.

Allwit said:

"Do thou think so, Davy?

"Then I am mortal, too. I am only a dead man, Davy. This is no world for me. Whenever he goes, I must necessarily truss up all — that is, pack everything up — and go after him, Davy. A sheet with two knots, and away."

The sheet was a shroud, aka a winding sheet; it was tied with a knot at the top and the bottom.

Or it was an improvised noose with which Allwit could truss himself — tie around his neck and use to hang himself.

Two servants led in Sir Walter, who had been hurt in the duel.

"O see, sir, how faint he goes," Davy said. "Two of my fellows lead him."

"O me!" Mistress Allwit said.

Allwit said:

"Heyday, my wife's laid low, too. Here's likely to be a good house kept when we are altogether down."

He was sarcastic.

Allwit continued:

"Take pains with her, good Davy, cheer her up there. Let me come to his worship, let me come."

"Don't touch me, villain," Sir Walter said to Allwit. "My wound aches at thee, thou poison to my heart."

Allwit said:

"He raves already. His senses are quite gone; he does not know me.

"Look up if it pleases your worship. Heave those eyes.

"Recall me to your mind. Is your remembrance lost?

"Look in my face. Who am I, if it pleases your worship?"

"If anything is worse than a slave or a villain, thou are the man," Sir Walter said.

Sir Walter knew very well who and what Allwit was.

"Alas, it's his poor worship's weakness," Allwit said. "He will begin to know me by little and little."

"No devil can be like thee," Sir Walter said.

Allwit said, "Ah, poor gentleman, I think the pain that thou endure —"

Sir Walter said:

"Thou know me to be wicked, for thy baseness kept the eyes open always on all my sins. None knew the dear account that my soul stood charged with as well as thou, yet like Hell's flattering fallen angel, thou would never tell me about it. Thou let me go on and join with death in sleep, with the result that if I had not waked now and become aware of my sinful state by chance, even by a stranger's pity, I had everlastingly slept out all hope of grace and mercy."

The stranger was Touchwood Junior, who had wounded Sir Walter, thus causing him to examine his life and become aware of his sins.

Hell's flattering fallen angel is Lucifer, who flatters people so they will commit evil.

The "dear account" is the account of one's life, including sins and good deeds.

"Now he is worse and worse," Allwit said. "Wife, go to him, wife. Thou were accustomed to do good on him."

One meaning of "do" is "have sex."

"How is it with you, sir?" Mistress Allwit asked Sir Walter.

Sir Walter said:

"Not as with you, thou loathsome strumpet.

"Some good pitying man, remove my sins out of my sight a little. I tremble to look at her. She keeps back all comfort while she stays.

"Is this a time, unconscionable — without a conscience — woman, to see thee? Are thou so cruel to the peace of man, not to give liberty — freedom from sin — now?

"The devil himself shows a far fairer reverence and respect to goodness than thyself. He dares not do this but departs in time of penitence and hides his face. When man withdraws from him, he leaves the place. Have thou less manners, and more impudence, than thy instructor — the devil himself?

"Please show thy modesty, if the least grain of modesty is left to thee and get thee away from me.

"Thou should be rather locked many rooms away from here, away from the poor miserable sight of me, if either love or grace had part in thee."

"He is lost forever," Mistress Allwit said.

False. Unrepentant sinners are lost forever. Sir Walter was repenting his sins.

"Run, sweet Davy, quickly, and bring the children here — the sight of them will make him cheerful right away," Allwit said.

Davy exited.

Sir Walter said to Mistress Allwit:

"O death! Is this a place for you to weep? What tears are those? Get you away with them! I shall fare the worse as long as the tears are weeping; they work against me. There's nothing but thy sexual appetite in that sorrow. Thou weep because of lust; I feel it in the slackness — the slowness — of spiritual comforts coming towards me.

"I was well until thou began to undo and ruin me. This looks like the fruitless sorrow of a careless mother who brings her son with dalliance — with over-indulgence — to the gallows, and then stands by, and weeps to see him suffer."

Davy returned with the children.

He said, "There are the children, sir, if it pleases your worship. Your most recent fine girl, truly, she smiles. Look, look, indeed, sir."

Sir Walter said:

"O these are God's vengeance on me. Let me forever hide my cursed face from the sight of those who darken all my hopes and stand between me and the sight of Heaven."

His children were the result of his sexual sins.

Sir Walter continued:

"Whoever sees me now, and sees her also, and sees those children so near me, may rightly say that I am overgrown with sin.

"O how my offences wrestle with my repentance, which can scarcely breath. Still my adulterous guilt hovers aloft, and with her black wings beats down all my prayers before they are halfway up to heaven. Who is he who knows now how long I have to live? O, what comes then?

"My taste grows bitter; the round world is all bitter gall to me now. The round world's pleasing pleasures that I exchanged my soul for now have poisoned me.

"May a hundred sighs of repentance at once make a way to Heaven for me."

"Speak to him, Nick," Allwit said.

"I don't dare," Nick said. "I am afraid."

"Tell him he hurts his wounds and makes them worse, Wat, with moaning and complaining," Allwit said.

"Wretched, death of seven!" Sir Walter said.

He had fathered seven children with Mistress Allwit. Because they were bastards, he worried that they would suffer spiritual death and suffer anguish like the anguish he was suffering.

Allwit said:

"Come, let's be talking about something that will keep him alive.

"Ah, sirrah Wat, and did my lord bestow that jewel on thee, for an epistle thou created in Latin?

"Thou are a good, forward — promising — boy; there's great joy on thee."

"O sorrow!" Sir Walter said.

Allwit said:

"By God's heart, will nothing comfort him?

"If he is so far gone, it is time to moan. Here's pen, and ink, and paper, and all things ready. Will it please your worship to make your will?"

"My will?" Sir Walter said. "Yes, yes, what else? Who writes apace — quickly — now?"

The word "will" means "lust," so it seemed appropriate to Sir Walter for him to make his last will and testament.

"That can your serving-man Davy, if it pleases your worship," Allwit said. "He has a fair, fast, legible hand."

Sir Walter said:

"Set my will down then:

"*Imprimis*, I bequeath to yonder wittol, three times his weight in curses —"

Imprimis is Latin for "in the first place."

Allwit said, "What!"

Sir Walter continued, "— all plagues of body and of mind —"

Allwit said, "Don't write that down, Davy."

"It is his will," Davy said. "I must write it down."

It is his will and testament — and it is what he wants.

Sir Walter continued, "— together also, with such a sickness, ten days before his death."

Sir Walter bequeathed to Allwit a long, painful death.

"There's a 'sweet' legacy," Allwit said. "I am almost choked with it."

Sir Walter then said:

"Next I bequeath to that foul whore, his wife, all barrenness of joy, a drought of virtue, and dearth of all repentance."

Sir Walter bequeathed to Mistress Allwit a lack of spiritual health.

Sir Walter then said to Mistress Allwit:

"And for her end and death, I bequeath to you the common misery of an English strumpet, in French and Dutch, beholding before she dies confusion — death and destruction — of her brats before her eyes, and never shed a tear for it."

If Mistress Allwit were to die before she repented her sins, she would be damned to Hell.

In this context, "French" means syphilis, and "Dutch" may mean gonorrhea.

"Dutch widow" was slang for "prostitute."

In Thomas Middleton's *A Trick to Catch the Old One*, a Dutch widow is called an English drab. A drab is 1) a dirty or untidy woman, 2) a prostitute, or 3) a promiscuous woman.

A servant entered the scene.

"Where's the knight?" the servant asked. "O sir, the gentleman you wounded is newly departed."

"Dead?" Sir Walter said. "Lift me! Lift me! Who helps me?"

Killing a man in a duel was a hanging offense.

"Let the law lift you now, the law that must have all," Allwit said. "I have finished lifting on you, and my wife, too."

A murderer's wealth was forfeit.

"Lift" can mean 1) help, 2) rob, and/or 3) have sex with.

When sexually aroused, a penis lifts itself.

"It would be best for you to lock yourself away in a secret place," the servant said.

"Not in my house, sir," Allwit said. "I'll harbor no such persons as men-slayers. Lock yourself wherever else you want."

"What's this!" Sir Walter said.

"Why, husband!" Mistress Allwit said.

"I know what I am doing, wife," Allwit said.

"You cannot tell yet what will happen," Mistress Allwit said. "Because he killed the man in self-defense, neither his life nor his estate will be touched, husband."

Sir Walter may yet be able to pay the Allwits' bills for a while.

"Go away, wife," Allwit said. "I hear a fool — thou! His lands will hang him."

In other words: People who want to seize Sir Walter's lands and wealth will make sure that he hangs.

"Am I denied a chamber?" Sir Walter said. "What do you say, indeed?"

He wanted to hide in Allwit's house.

Mistress Allwit said to Sir Walter:

"Alas, sir, I am one who would have all well, but I must obey my husband."

She then said to her husband:

"Please, love, let the poor gentleman stay, being so badly wounded. There's a secluded chamber at one end of the garret we never use. Let him have that, I request of you."

Allwit said:

"We never use it!

"You forget sickness then, and physic times — times when medicine is needed."

It was perhaps used as an isolation chamber when plague was present.

Or it was a place when a sick person could vomit.

Allwit then asked:

"Isn't it a place for easement?"

It was a place to ease the body: to pass urine and excrement. It was a privy.

"O death!" Sir Walter said. "Do I hear this with part of former life in me?"

A second servant entered the scene.

Sir Walter asked the servant:

"What's the news now?

"Indeed, the news is worse and worse," the second servant said. "You're likely to lose your land even if the law saves your life, sir, or the surgeon."

"Listen to that there, wife," Allwit said.

"Why, what, sir?" Sir Walter said.

"Sir Oliver Kix' wife is newly quickened," the second servant said. "She's pregnant. That child undoes and ruins you, sir."

The Kixes' child would inherit the land that Sir Walter was expecting to inherit.

"All ill news all at once," Sir Walter said.

Allwit said:

"I wonder what Sir Walter is doing here with his consorts — his companions?

"Cannot our house be private to ourselves, but we must have such guests?

"I ask you to depart, sirs, and take your murderer along with you — it would be good if he were apprehended before he left. He's killed some honest gentleman; send for officers."

"I'll soon save you that labor," Sir Walter said.

He would leave soon.

"I must tell you, sir, that you have been somewhat bolder in my house than I could well like of," Allwit said. "I endured you until it stuck here at my heart. I tell you truly that I thought you had been familiar with my wife once."

He was pretending to be shocked — shocked, he tells you! — that Sir Walter had had sex with his wife once.

"With me?" Mistress Allwit said. "I'll see him hanged first; I defy him, and all such gentlemen in the like extremity."

She was pretending to be shocked — shocked, she tells you! — that anyone thought that Sir Walter had had sex with her once.

Sir Walter said:

"If ever eyes were open, these — my eyes — are they.

"Gamesters, farewell, I have nothing left to play."

"Gamesters" are 1) gamblers, and/or 2) lechers.

He exited.

"And therefore, get you gone, sir," Allwit said.

Davy said to Allwit:

"Of all wittols, be thou the head — the paragon."

Davy then said to Mistress Allwit:

"And thou, be the grand whore of spitals."

"Spitals" were places where venereal disease was treated.

Davy and the two servants exited.

"So, since he's likely now to be rid of all his lands and wealth, I am very glad that I am so well rid of him," Allwit said.

"I knew that he did not dare to stay, when you named officers," Mistress Allwit said.

Allwit said:

"That stopped his spirits immediately."

He then asked:

"What shall we do now, wife?"

"As we were accustomed to do," Mistress Allwit said.

"We are richly furnished, wife, with household stuff," Allwit said.

"Let's rent out lodgings then, and take a house in the Strand," Mistress Allwit said.

The Strand was a fashionable area, but it was also known for high-class prostitutes.

The Allwits could start a high-class brothel where prostitutes stayed.

Allwit said:

"In truth, it's a match, wench. It's an agreement: I agree.

"We are absolutely stocked with cloth-of-tissue cushions, to furnish out bay windows."

"Cloth-of-tissue cushions" had threads of silver and gold woven into the cushions.

Prostitutes sat in bay windows to display themselves to prospective customers.

Allwit continued:

"Bah, what is there that isn't quaint and costly, from the top to the bottom?"

The word "quaint" means "fashionable." The word was also used to mean "cunt."

Allwit continued:

"By God's life, as for furniture, we may lodge a countess."

Elizabethan and Jacobean playwrights often used the word "countess" to pun on "cunt."

"There's a close stool of tawny velvet, too, now that I think of it, wife."

A close stool is a chamber pot in a stool or a box.

"There's everything there ought to be, sir," Mistress Allwit said. "Your nose must be in everything."

Including a close-stool.

Allwit said:

"I have finished, wench."

The Allwits were going to set up a high-class brothel.

Probably, that was what they did before Sir Walter began to pay their bills.

Allwit continued:

"And let this sign be posted in every gallant's chamber:

"There is no gamester [gambler or lecher] like a politic sinner,

"For whoever games [gambles or leches], the box is sure to be a winner."

A politic sinner knows when to quit.

The box held the money that went to the gambling house or brothal.

"Box" is also a word that means "coffin."

Allwit felt that whatever role he played — wittol or proprietor of a brothel — he would get money.

Sir Walter had been a gamester — a lecher. It seemed that Sir Walter would lose everything, including his life, but Allwit would still have costly furnishings.

Allwit and Mistress Allwit exited.

Yellowhammer and his wife talked together about Moll, who was ill, in their house.

"O husband, husband, she will die! She will die!" Maudlin said. "There is no sign but death."

"It will be our shame then," Yellowhammer said.

"O, how she's changed in the compass — the passage — of an hour!" Maudlin said.

"Ah, my poor girl!" Yellowhammer said. "In good faith, thou were too cruel to drag her by the hair."

"You would have done as much, sir, to curb her of her humor," Maudlin said.

Moll's "humor" was her disposition to run away and marry Touchwood Junior.

"It is curbed sweetly," Yellowhammer said sarcastically. "She caught her bane — death — of the water."

Moll had fallen into the water.

And she had caught her bane of Sir Walter.

Tim entered the scene.

"How are things now, Tim?" Maudlin asked.

"Indeed, I am busy, mother, writing an epitaph upon my sister's death," Tim said.

"Death!" Maudlin said. "She is not dead, I hope."

"No," Tim said, "but she intends to be, and that's as good, and when a thing's done, it is done. You taught me that, mother."

Moll wanted to die.

"What is your tutor doing?" Yellowhammer asked.

"He is creating an epitaph, too, in principal — that is, excellent — pure Latin, culled out of Ovid: *de Tristibus*."

Ovid's *Tristia* was a collection of sad poems written after Caesar Augustus had exiled him.

"How does your sister look?" Yellowhammer asked. "Hasn't she changed?"

"Changed?" Tim said. "Gold into white money was never so changed as is my sister's color into paleness."

White money is silver money.

Moll entered the scene.

"O, here she's brought," Yellowhammer said. "See how she looks like death."

"She looks like death, and I have not written a word yet!" Tim said. "I must go beat my brains against a bed post and beget an epitaph before my tutor does."

Tim exited.

"Speak," Yellowhammer said to Moll. "How are thou doing?"

"I hope I shall be well, for I am as sick at heart as I can be," Moll said.

"Alas, my poor girl," Yellowhammer said. "The doctor's making a most sovereign drink for thee. The worst — that is, the least expensive — ingredients are dissolved pearl and amber. We spare no cost, girl."

"Your love comes too late, yet my timely thanks reward it," Moll said. "What is comfort when the poor patient's heart is past relief? No doctor's art can cure my grief."

Yellowhammer said:

"All is cast away then."

In other words: He had wasted the money that was spent on the expensive medicine.

Yellowhammer then said to Moll:

"Please, look upon me cheerfully."

Maudlin said:

"Sing but a strain or two. Thou will not believe how it will revive thy spirits. Strive with thy fit."

"Fit" can mean 1) illness, or 2) a part of a song.

Maudlin continued:

"Please, sweet Moll."

"You shall have my good will, Mother," Moll said.

"Why, well said, wench," Maudlin said.

Moll sang:

"*Weep eyes, break heart,*

"*My love and I must part*;

"*Cruel fates true love do soonest sever,*

"O, I shall see thee, never, never, never.

"O, happy is the maid [maiden] whose life takes end,

"Ere [Before] it knows parent's frown, or loss of friend [lover].

"Weep eyes, break heart,

"My love and I must part."

Carrying a letter, Touchwood Senior entered the scene.

"O, I could die with music," Maudlin said. "Well sung, girl."

"If you call it well sung, it was," Moll said.

"She plays the swan and sings herself to death," Yellowhammer said.

According to a folk belief, swans were thought to sing as they died.

"By your leave, sir," Touchwood Senior said.

He wanted to attract Yellowhammer's attention.

"Who are you, sir?" Yellowhammer asked. "And what's your business, please tell me?"

"I may be admitted," Touchwood Senior said. "Although I am the brother of him whom your hate pursued, the hatred spreads no further. Your malice sets in death, doesn't it, sir?"

Like the sun setting, the hatred of a person declines and dies when that person dies.

"In death?" Yellowhammer asked.

"My brother is dead," Touchwood Senior said. "His love of Moll was a dear love to him. It cost him just his life — that was all, sir. He paid enough, poor gentleman, for his love."

Yellowhammer said to himself:

"There's all our ills removed, if only Moll were well now."

Yellowhammer then said to Touchwood Senior:

"Impute not, sir, his end to any hate that sprung from us; he had a fair wound that brought about his death."

Sir Walter had wounded Touchwood Junior in a duel.

Touchwood Senior said:

"That helped him go forward to his death, I must necessarily confess.

"But the restraint of love, and your unkindness — those were the wounds that from his heart drew blood. But being past help, let words forget it, too.

"Scarcely three minutes before his eyelids closed and took eternal leave of this world's light, he wrote this letter, which by oath he bound me to give to her — his loved one's — own hands. That's all my business here."

"You may perform your business now then," Yellowhammer said. "There she sits."

"O, with a following look," Touchwood Senior said.

Moll looked ill, as if she would follow Touchwood Junior in death.

"Aye, trust me, sir," Yellowhammer said. "I think she'll follow him quickly."

"Here's some gold he told me to distribute faithfully among your servants," Touchwood Senior said.

He wanted to reward Susan, who had helped Moll. By giving some money to all the Yellowhammer servants, he would not draw special attention to Susan.

"Alas, what does he mean, sir?" Yellowhammer asked.

This was a polite protest meaning, "He shouldn't have!"

"How are you, mistress?" Touchwood Senior asked Moll.

"I must learn that from you, sir," Moll said.

Touchwood Junior's letter to her would either cheer her up or dishearten her.

"Here's a letter from a friend of yours," Touchwood Senior said, "and where that fails in satisfaction, I have a sad tongue ready to supply what is missing in the letter."

"Tell me how he is before I look at the letter," Moll said.

"Seldom better," Touchwood Senior said. "He has a contented health now."

"I am most glad of it," Moll said.

She began to read the letter.

"Is he dead, sir?" Maudlin asked quietly.

"He is," Yellowhammer said quietly. "Now, wife, let's just get the girl upon her legs again, and let's get her to church promptly."

"O, he tells me that he is sick to death," Moll said, reading the letter. "How is he doing after writing this letter?"

"Indeed, he feels no pain at all," Touchwood Senior said. "He's dead, sweet mistress."

"May peace close my eyes," Moll said.

She swooned.

"The girl," Yellowhammer said. "Look to the girl, wife."

"Moll, daughter," Maudlin said. "Sweet girl, speak. Look up just once. Thou shall have all the wishes of thy heart that wealth can purchase."

"O, she's gone forever," Yellowhammer said. "That letter broke her heart."

"As good die now, then, as let her lie in torment, and then break it," Touchwood Senior said.

Susan, Moll's chambermaid, entered the scene.

"O Susan, she whom thou loved so dearly is gone," Maudlin said.

"Is gone" meant "is dead."

"O sweet maiden!" Susan said.

Touchwood Senior said to himself:

"This is she who helped Moll always."

Susan had helped Moll escape over the rooftops.

He then said to her:

"I've a reward here for thee."

He gave her some money.

"Take her — Moll — in," Yellowhammer said. "Remove her from our sight, our shame, and our sorrow."

He wanted Moll's body to be removed from the room.

"Wait, let me help thee," Touchwood Senior said. "It is the last cold kindness I can perform for my sweet brother's sake."

Touchwood Senior and Susan, carrying Moll, exited the scene.

"All the whole street will hate us, and the world will point me out as a cruel father," Yellowhammer said. "It is our best course of action, wife, after we have given order for the funeral, to absent ourselves until she is laid in the ground."

"Where shall we spend that time?" Maudlin asked.

"I'll tell thee where, wench," Yellowhammer said. "Go to some private — secluded — church and marry Tim to the rich Brecknock gentlewoman."

The rich Brecknock gentlewoman was the Welsh gentlewoman.

"By the mass, a marriage match," Maudlin said. "Agreed! We'll not lose everything at once; something we'll catch."

Tim would get the Welsh gentlewoman's dowry.

Yellowhammer and Maudlin exited.

Sir Oliver and some servants were in Sir Oliver's house.

Sir Oliver said:

"Ho, my wife's quickened — she's pregnant! I am a man forever; I think I have bestirred my stumps, indeed."

And bestirred his penis.

According to the *Oxford English Dictionary*, "to stir one's stumps" means "to do one's duty zealously."

Sir Oliver continued:

"Run, get your fellows all together instantly, then go to the parish church and ring the bells."

The church bells rang when important news was announced.

"It shall be done, sir," the first servant said.

The first servant exited.

"Upon my love I charge you, villain, that you make a bonfire before the door at night," Sir Oliver ordered.

A "villain" is a servant.

"A bonfire, sir?" the second servant asked.

Bonfires were also lit when important news was announced.

"A thwacking one, I charge you," Sir Oliver said.

"Thwacking" means "big."

"This is monstrous," the second servant said.

The second servant may have been aware that Sir Oliver had been cuckolded. Or he may have thought that Lady Kix' pregnancy was not important enough to be announced with the ringing of church bells and with a bonfire.

The second servant exited.

Sir Oliver said to the third servant, "Run and count a hundred pounds out for the gentleman who gave my wife the drink, the first thing you do."

"A hundred pounds, sir?" the third servant said.

It was a lot of money.

Sir Oliver said:

"A bargain. As our joy grows, we must remember still from whence it flows, or else we prove ungrateful multipliers.

"The child is coming, and the land comes afterward. The news of this will make a poor Sir Walter.

"I have struck it home, indeed."

"Struck it home" means 1) hit the center of the target with an arrow, and 2) hit my wife's vagina with an "arrow."

The third servant said:

"That you have, by the Virgin Mary, sir.

"But will your worship be going to the funeral of both these lovers?"

The two lovers were Touchwood Junior and Moll.

"Both? Both go together?" Sir Oliver asked. "There will be one funeral?"

"Aye, sir," the third servant said. "The gentleman's brother — Touchwood Senior — will have it so. It will be the pitifullest sight. There's such running, such rumors, and such throngs. A pair of lovers never had more spectators, more men's pities, or more women's wet eyes."

"My wife helps increase the number of mourners then?" Sir Oliver asked.

"There's such a drawing out of handkerchiefs, and those who have no handkerchiefs lift up aprons," the third servant said.

"Her parents may have 'joyful' hearts at this," Sir Oliver said. "I would not have my cruelty to any child of mine so talked about, for a monopoly."

Monopolies were very profitable.

"I believe you, sir," the third servant said. "It is cast — arranged — so, too, that both their coffins will meet, which will be lamentable."

"Come, we'll go and see it," Sir Oliver said.

He and the third servant exited.

Recorders played dolefully in a church.

From one door entered the solemnly arrayed coffin of the gentleman — Touchwood Junior — his sword upon the coffin, attended by many people in black, including Sir Oliver, Allwit, and a parson. His brother — Touchwood Senior — was the chief mourner.

From the other door entered the coffin of the virgin — Moll — with a garland of flowers, with epitaphs pinned on it, attended by maidens and women, including Lady Kix, Mistress Allwit, and Susan.

The epitaphs were those of Tim and his tutor.

The coffin bearers set the coffins down one alongside the other, while all wept and mourned.

A sad song came from the music room.

Touchwood Senior said:

"Never could death boast of a richer prize from the first parent: Adam.

"I challenge the world to bring forth a pair of truer hearts.

"To speak only truth about this departed gentleman, in a brother, might by hard censure — critical judgment — be called flattery, which makes me rather silent in his right than so to be delivered to the thoughts of any envious hearer starved and lacking in virtue, and therefore repining and feeling unhappy when he hears that others thrive.

"But as for this maiden, whom envy cannot hurt with all her poisons, having left to ages the true, chaste monuments of her living name, which no time can deface, I say the full truth freely about her, without fear of censure.

"What nature could there shine, which might redeem perfection home to woman, only in her was fully glorious."

Moll was so virtuous that she could redeem for women the perfection that Eve had lost with her disobedience in the Garden of Eden.

Touchwood Senior continued:

"Beauty set like a jewel in goodness expresses what she was — that jewel was so infixed in her.

"There was no lack of anything of life to make these virtuous precedents man and wife."

Touchwood Junior and Moll were examples whom other men and women ought to follow.

"I feel great pity about their deaths," Allwit said.

"We never felt more pity than now," one of the mourners said.

"It makes a hundred weeping eyes, sweet gossip," Lady Kix said.

"I cannot think that there's anyone among you, in this full fair assembly, maiden, man, or wife, whose heart would not have sprung with joy and gladness to have seen their marriage day," Touchwood Senior said.

"It would have made a thousand joyful hearts," one of the mourners said.

Touchwood Senior said to the "corpses" of Touchwood Junior and Moll, "Get up then quickly, and take your fortunes. Make these hearts joyful. Here is no one but friends."

Moll and Touchwood Junior rose from their coffins.

"Alive, sir!" one of the people present said. "O sweet, dear couple."

Touchwood Senior said:

"Nay, do not hinder them now. Stand back away from them. If she should be caught again and have this time — this opportunity — taken away from her, I'll never plot further for them, nor will this honest chambermaid who helped all at a push."

"At a push" means "in an emergency," but "push" also referred to the act of sex.

Touchwood Junior said to the parson, "Good sir, quickly."

He wanted to be married quickly to Moll.

The parson said:

"Hands join now, but hearts forever,

"Which no parent's mood shall sever."

That mood would be anger.

The parson said to Touchwood Junior:

"You shall forsake all widows, wives, and maid[en]s."

The parson then said to Moll:

"You, [You shall forsake] lords, knights, gentlemen, and men of trades."

The parson then said to both of them:

"And if in haste, any article misses,

"Go interline it with a brace [a pair] of kisses."

An "article" is a contractual clause in the wedding vows.

"Interline" means "write in."

Touchwood Senior said:

"Here's a thing trolled nimbly."

"Trolled nimbly" means "uttered swiftly."

Touchwood Senior continued:

"May God give you joy, brother. Isn't it better that thou should have her than that the maiden should die?"

"Joy to you, sweet mistress bride," Mistress Allwit said.

"Joy, joy to you both," some of the people present said.

"Here are your wedding sheets that you brought along with you," Touchwood Senior said. "You may both go to bed when you please."

The wedding sheets were the shrouds.

"My joy wants — lacks — utterance," Touchwood Junior said. "My joy is beyond speech."

"Utter all at night then, brother," Touchwood Senior said.

In other words: Make sounds of delight while having sex.

One meaning of "utter" is "shoot out or discharge."

Touchwood Junior could utter sounds of delight while uttering semen.

"I am silent with delight," Moll said.

Touchwood Senior said, "Sister, delight will silence any woman, but you'll find your tongue again among maidservants, now that you keep house, sister."

Many of the women with whom Touchwood Senior had sex with stayed silent about it for fear of injuring their reputations. But Moll was now a married woman and she could use her tongue while having sex with her husband and she could tell her friends about it later.

And if Moll is silent during sex with her husband, she will find her tongue as a housewife when she 1) loudly criticizes the maidservants, and/or 2) has sex with the maidservants.

"Never was an hour so filled with joy and wonder," one of the people present said.

"To tell you the full story of this chambermaid, and of her kindness in this business to us, it would ask an hour's discourse," Touchwood Senior said. "In brief, it was she who wrought it to this purpose cunningly."

See why we should value female brains?

"We shall all love her for it," one of the people present said.

Yellowhammer and his wife, Maudlin, entered the scene.

"See who comes here now," one of the people present said.

"A storm, a storm, but we are sheltered for it," Touchwood Senior said.

Touchwood Junior and Moll were legally married.

Yellowhammer said, "I will anticipate you all, and mock you — you and your expectation — thus: I stand happy, both in your lives, and in your hearts' combination."

Yellowhammer and his wife had reason to be happy: Their daughter, Moll, was alive!

Touchwood Junior and Moll were already married, and Yellowhammer was willing to accept that marriage.

"Here's a strange day again," Touchwood Senior said.

Yellowhammer said:

"The knight — Sir Walter — has proved to be a villain. All's come out now. His niece is an arrant baggage. My poor boy, Tim, is cast away this morning, even before breakfast. He married a whore next to his heart."

"A whore?" all asked.

"Sir Walter's niece, indeed," Yellowhammer said.

"I think we rid our hands in good time of him," Allwit said to his wife.

Mistress Allwit replied:

"I knew he was past the best, when I gave him over."

She then asked Yellowhammer:

"What has become of him, please, sir?"

Yellowhammer said:

"Who, the knight?

"He lies — lodges — in the knight's ward now."

Sir Walter had been arrested for debt. He had borrowed money with the expectation that he would inherit the Kixes' land. Now that Lady Kix was pregnant with an heir, Sir Walter's creditors had had him arrested because of his debts.

Although he was in prison for his debts, he had repented his sins.

The knight's ward was a section of the debtors' prison.

Yellowhammer then said to Lady Kix:

"Your belly, lady, begins to blossom, and so there's no peace for Sir Walter — his creditors are so greedy."

Sir Oliver said to Touchwood Senior:

"Mr. Touchwood, do thou hear this news?

"I am so endeared to thee for my wife's fruitfulness that I charge you both, your wife and thee, to live no more apart from each other and face the world's frowns.

"I have purse, and bed, and board for you."

Mistress Touchwood was living with her uncle because Touchwood Senior had been unable to provide for her.

The world frowns when a husband is unable to provide for his wife.

But the world would frown if it knew that Touchwood Senior was living in Sir Oliver's house while cuckolding him.

"Don't be afraid to go to your business roundly. Beget children, and I'll keep them."

"Roundly" means "with vigor." It also calls to mind the round bellies of pregnant women.

"Do you say so, sir?" Touchwood Senior asked.

"Test me, with three at a birth, if thou dare now," Sir Oliver said.

In other words: I dare you to get triplets. I'll approve of it.

The triplets could be birthed by Touchwood Senior's wife or by Sir Oliver's wife.

"Take heed how you dare a man, while you live, sir, who has good skill with his weapon," Touchwood Senior said.

His "weapon" was below his belly button.

"By God's foot, I dare you to, sir," Sir Oliver said.

Tim, his tutor, and Tim's newly wedded wife — the Welsh gentlewoman — entered the scene.

Seeing them, Yellowhammer said, "Look, gentlemen. If ever you saw the picture of the unfortunate marriage, yonder it is."

The Welsh gentlewoman, who had been expostulating with her husband, said, "Nay, good, sweet Tim —"

Tim interrupted, "Come from the university, to marry a whore in London, with my tutor, too? *O tempora! O mors!*"

["Oh, the times! Oh, death!"]

Cicero wrote, "*O tempora! O mores!*"

["Oh, the times! Oh, the customs and manners!"]

[In other words: "What is the world coming to!"]

Tim's tutor said, "Please, Tim, be patient."

Tim said:

"I bought a jade at Cambridge."

A "jade" is a bad horse. It is also a word used to insult a woman: It can be used to mean "whore."

Since Tim bought a jade at Cambridge, he did not want to make another mistake and have a jade for a wife.

Tim continued:

"I'll let her out to execution — I'll hire her out so she can pay her debt (the lack of a dowry) to me — tutor, for eighteen pence a day, or let her out to the Brentford horse races. She'll serve to carry seven miles out of town well."

The word "horse" was sometimes used to call to mind the word "whore."

Tim was talking about pimping his wife to make money.

He then said to the Welsh gentlewoman:

"Where are these mountains? I was promised mountains, but there's such a *mist*, I can see none of them."

Tim had *missed* marrying a woman with a dowry.

Tim continued:

"What has become of those two thousand runts?

"Let's have a bout with them in the meantime."

In other words: Let's have an argument about them in the meantime.

Tim continued:

"May a vengeance runt — reprove — thee."

"Good, sweet Tim, have patience," Maudlin said.

Tim said, "*Flectere si nequeo superos, Acheronta movebo*, mother."

["Since I cannot move the powers above, I will work on (the powers of) the lower regions."]

The "lower regions" are 1) the Underworld, and 2) the regions below the belly button.

The Latin is from Virgil's *Aeneid*, Book 7, line 312.

Maudlin said:

"I think you have married her in logic, Tim.

"You told me once that by logic you would prove that a whore is an honest woman. Now prove that she is an honest woman, Tim, and take her for thy labor."

An honest woman is a chaste woman.

He could physically "labor" with her under him in bed.

That would be his reward for his intellectual labor in proving that the Welsh gentlewoman is honest.

Tim said:

"Truly, I thank you.

"I grant to you that I may prove another man's wife to be an honest woman, but not my own."

"There's no remedy now, Tim," Maudlin said. "You must prove her to be honest as well as you may."

Tim and the Welsh gentlewoman were legally married. Getting a divorce would be very difficult. It was better to make the best of a bad situation.

Tim said:

"Why, then my tutor and I will do so about her, as well as we can."

The word "do" can mean "have sex with."

Tim continued:

"*Uxor non est meretrix, ergo falacis.*"

["A wife is not a whore; therefore, you (who say she is) are wrong."]

"Sir, if your logic cannot prove me honest," the Welsh gentlewoman said, "there's a thing called marriage, and that makes me honest."

"O, there's a trick beyond your logic, Tim," Maudlin said.

Actually, Tim and the Welsh gentlewoman were making the same argument.

The trick was a merry trick.

The Latin word for "whore" is *meretrix*.

Tim said:

"I perceive then that a woman may be honest according to the English print and spelling [merry trick], when she is a whore [*meretrix*] in the Latin. So much for marriage and logic. I'll love her for her wit.

"I'll pick out my runts there."

His "runts" may be his future children.

Tim continued:

"And for my mountains, I'll mount upon —"

"Mount upon —"

Hmm.

Mount upon a *mons veneris*.

Yellowhammer said:

"So fortune seldom deals two marriages with one hand, and both lucky. The best thing is, one feast will serve them both.

"By the Virgin Mary, to have room enough for all, I'll have the dinner kept in Goldsmiths' Hall, to which, kind gallants, I invite you all."

You, the audience and readers, are kind gallants.

Goldsmiths' Hall is quite a distance away, so you are unlikely to arrive in time for the wedding feast,

This is a happy ending: two marriages, and Yellowhammer has to pay for only one wedding feast.

Everyone exited.

APPENDIX A: NOTES
— 2.2 —
Bill of Middlesex

For Your Information:

*The **Bill of Middlesex** was a legal fiction used by the Court of King's Bench to gain jurisdiction over cases traditionally in the remit of the Court of Common Pleas. Hinging on the King's Bench's remaining criminal jurisdiction over the county of Middlesex, the Bill allowed it to take cases traditionally in the remit of other common law courts by claiming that the defendant had committed trespass in Middlesex. Once the defendant was in custody, the trespass complaint would be quietly dropped and other complaints (such as debt or detinue) would be substituted.*

The bill was part of a large reform movement to prevent equitable courts such as the Court of Chancery from undermining their business. It was far cheaper and faster than the older equivalents used by the Chancery and Common Pleas, leading to a drop in their business and an increase in that of the King's Bench. As such, the Chancery issued injunctions in an ineffective attempt to prevent its use. The Bill was finally abolished by the Uniformity of Process Act 1832.

Source: "Bill of Middlesex." Wikipedia. Accessed 2 February 2023
https://en.wikipedia.org/wiki/Bill_of_Middlesex

— 2.2 —

Witch's Mark

For Your Information:

*The **witch's teat** was a raised bump somewhere on a witch's body. It is often depicted as having a wart-like appearance.*

Beliefs about the mark on witches

The witch's teat is associated with the perversion of maternal power by witches in early modern England. The witch's teat is associated with the feeding of witches' imps or familiars; the witch's familiar supposedly aided the witch in her magic in exchange for nourishment (blood) from sacrificial animals or from the witch's teat. It is also where the devil supposedly suckles when he comes at night to bed his faithful servants, sometimes impregnating them with his seed.

Source: "Witch's Mark." Wikipedia. Accessed 2 February 2023
https://en.wikipedia.org/wiki/Witch%27s_mark

— 2.2 —

Godparents

For Your Information:

How many godparents can a child have?

According to the Catholic Church, a child can have up to two godparents (and in that case, they must be a man and woman), but only one is required. But as Bos points out, each church or organization may have their own unique guidelines. "Traditionally it's been two, but some churches have three, some only have one and others have no specified number at all," he says. And of course, if you like the idea of naming non-religious godparents, you can have as many as you'd like.

Source: Stephanie Grassullo, "Your Guide to Picking Godparents: What They Do and How to Choose." The Bump. February 2019. Updated 8 May 2020.

https://www.thebump.com/a/what-is-a-godparent

For Your Information:

Below is a [Catholic] Canon Law citation regarding the selection of godparents.

Can. 872 – Insofar as possible, a person to be baptized is to be given a sponsor who assists an adult in Christian initiation or together with the parents presents an infant for baptism. A sponsor also helps the baptized person to lead a Christian life in keeping with baptism and to fulfill faithfully the obligations inherent in it.

Can. 873 – There is to be only one male sponsor or one female sponsor or one of each.

Can. 874 §1 – To be permitted to take on the function of sponsor a person must:

1. be designated by the one to be baptized, by the parents or the person who takes their place, or in their absence by the pastor or minister and have the aptitude and intention of fulfilling this function;

2. have completed the 16th year of age, unless the diocesan bishop has established another age, or the pastor or minister has granted an exception for a just cause;

3. be a Catholic who has been confirmed and has already received the most holy Sacrament of the Eucharist and who leads a life of faith in keeping with the function to be taken on;

4. not be bound by any canonical penalty legitimately imposed or declared;

5. not be the father or mother of the one to be baptized.

Source: "Choosing Godparents for Baby's Baptism." Diocese of Allentown. 2023
https://www.allentowndiocese.org/catholic-QandA/godparents
For Your Information:

*godparent, formally **sponsor (from Latin spondere, "to promise")**, masculine **godfather**, feminine **godmother**, in Christianity, one who stands surety for another in the rite of baptism. In the modern baptism of an infant or child, the godparent or godparents make a profession of faith for the person being baptized (the godchild) and assume an obligation to serve as proxies for the parents if the parents either are unable or neglect to provide for the religious training of the child, in fulfillment of baptismal promises. Even when the parents provide their child with a religious upbringing, a godparent serves to encourage the child's spiritual growth over time and stands as an example of another adult with maturity in the faith. In churches mandating a sponsor, only one godparent is required; two (in most churches, of different sex) are permitted. Many Protestant denominations permit but do not* *require godparents to join the infant's natural parents as sponsors. In the Roman Catholic Church, godparents must be of the Catholic faith.*

Source: "godparent." Britannica. Last updated: 10 February 2023
https://www.britannica.com/topic/godparent

— 4.1 —

Distichs of Cato

For Your Information:

*The **Distichs of Cato** (Latin: Catonis Disticha, most famously known simply as **Cato**), is a Latin collection of proverbial wisdom and morality by an unknown author from the 3rd or 4th century AD. The Cato was the most popular medieval schoolbook for teaching Latin, prized not only as a Latin textbook, but as a moral compass. Cato was in common use as a Latin teaching aid as late as the 18th century, used by Benjamin Franklin. It was one of the best-known books in the Middle Ages and was translated into many languages.*

Source: "*Distichs of Cato.*" Wikipedia. Accessed 10 March 2023
https://en.wikipedia.org/wiki/Distichs_of_Cato

— 4.4 —

Ovid's Ars Amatoria

Ovid's *Ars Amatoria*, Book 2, lines 243-246 states:

> *Si tibi per tutum planumque negabitur ire,*
> *Atque erit opposita ianua fulta sera,*
> *At tu per praeceps tecto delabere aperto:*
> *Det quoque furtivas alta fenestra vias.*

http://www.perseus.tufts.edu/hopper/
text?doc=Perseus%3Atext%3A1999.02.0069%3Atext%3DArs%3Abook%3D2

English Translation
Learn this ye lovers, and renounce your pride.
When all access is to your mistress hard,
When ev'ry door's secur'd, and window barr'd,
The roof untile, some desp'rate passage find;

Source: P. Ovidius Naso. *Ovid's Art of Love* (in three Books), the Remedy of Love, the Art of Beauty, the Court of Love, the History of Love, and Amours. Anne Mahoney. edited for Perseus. New York. Calvin Blanchard. 1855.
http://www.perseus.tufts.edu/hopper/
text?doc=Perseus%3Atext%3A1999.02.0069%3Atext%3DArs%3Abook%3D2

APPENDIX B: FAIR USE

§ 107. Limitations on exclusive rights: Fair use
    Release date: 2004-04-30

Notwithstanding the provisions of sections 106 and 106A, the fair use of a copyrighted work, including such use by reproduction in copies or phonorecords or by any other means specified by that section, for purposes such as criticism, comment, news reporting, teaching (including multiple copies for classroom use), scholarship, or research, is not an infringement of copyright. In determining whether the use made of a work in any particular case is a fair use the factors to be considered shall include —

(1) the purpose and character of the use, including whether such use is of a commercial nature or is for nonprofit educational purposes;

(2) the nature of the copyrighted work;

(3) the amount and substantiality of the portion used in relation to the copyrighted work as a whole; and

(4) the effect of the use upon the potential market for or value of the copyrighted work.

The fact that a work is unpublished shall not itself bar a finding of fair use if such finding is made upon consideration of all the above factors.

Source of Fair Use information:
http://www.law.cornell.edu/uscode/17/107.html

APPENDIX C: ABOUT THE AUTHOR

It was a dark and stormy night. Suddenly a cry rang out, and on a hot summer night in 1954, Josephine, wife of Carl Bruce, gave birth to a boy — me. Unfortunately, this young married couple allowed Reuben Saturday, Josephine's brother, to name their first-born. Reuben, aka "The Joker," decided that Bruce was a nice name, so he decided to name me Bruce Bruce. I have gone by my middle name — David — ever since.

Being named Bruce David Bruce hasn't been all bad. Bank tellers remember me very quickly, so I don't often have to show an ID. It can be fun in charades, also. When I was a counselor as a teenager at Camp Echoing Hills in Warsaw, Ohio, a fellow counselor gave the signs for "sounds like" and "two words," then she pointed to a bruise on her leg twice. Bruise Bruise? Oh yeah, Bruce Bruce is the answer!

Uncle Reuben, by the way, gave me a haircut when I was in kindergarten. He cut my hair short and shaved a small bald spot on the back of my head. My mother wouldn't let me go to school until the bald spot grew out again.

Of all my brothers and sisters (six in all), I am the only transplant to Athens, Ohio. I was born in Newark, Ohio, and have lived all around Southeastern Ohio. However, I moved to Athens to go to Ohio University and have never left.

At Ohio U, I never could make up my mind whether to major in English or Philosophy, so I got a bachelor's degree with a double major in both areas, then I added a Master of Arts degree in English and a Master of Arts degree in Philosophy. Yes, I have my MAMA degree.

Currently, and for a long time to come (I eat fruits and veggies), I am spending my retirement writing books such as *Nadia Comaneci: Perfect 10*, *The Funniest People in Comedy*, *Homer's* Iliad: *A Retelling in Prose*, and *William Shakespeare's* Hamlet: *A Retelling in Prose*.

If all goes well, I will publish one or two books a year for the rest of my life. (On the other hand, a good way to make God laugh is to tell Her your plans.)

By the way, my sister Brenda Kennedy writes romances such as *A New Beginning* and *Shattered Dreams*.

APPENDIX D: SOME BOOKS BY DAVID BRUCE

Retellings of a Classic Work of Literature

Arden of Faversham*: A Retelling*

Ben Jonson's The Alchemist: *A Retelling*

Ben Jonson's The Arraignment, or Poetaster: *A Retelling*

Ben Jonson's Bartholomew Fair: *A Retelling*

Ben Jonson's The Case is Altered: *A Retelling*

Ben Jonson's Catiline's Conspiracy: *A Retelling*

Ben Jonson's The Devil is an Ass: *A Retelling*

Ben Jonson's Epicene: *A Retelling*

Ben Jonson's Every Man in His Humor: *A Retelling*

Ben Jonson's Every Man Out of His Humor: *A Retelling*

Ben Jonson's The Fountain of Self-Love, or Cynthia's Revels: *A Retelling*

Ben Jonson's The Magnetic Lady, or Humors Reconciled: *A Retelling*

Ben Jonson's The New Inn, or The Light Heart: *A Retelling*

Ben Jonson's Sejanus' Fall: *A Retelling*

Ben Jonson's The Staple of News: *A Retelling*

Ben Jonson's A Tale of a Tub: *A Retelling*

Ben Jonson's Volpone, or the Fox: *A Retelling*

Christopher Marlowe's Complete Plays: Retellings

Christopher Marlowe's Dido, Queen of Carthage: *A Retelling*

Christopher Marlowe's Doctor Faustus: *Retellings of the 1604 A-Text and of the 1616 B-Text*

Christopher Marlowe's Edward II: *A Retelling*

Christopher Marlowe's The Massacre at Paris: *A Retelling*

Christopher Marlowe's The Rich Jew of Malta: *A Retelling*

Christopher Marlowe's Tamburlaine, Parts 1 and 2: *Retellings*

Dante's Divine Comedy: *A Retelling in Prose*

Dante's Inferno: *A Retelling in Prose*

Dante's Purgatory: *A Retelling in Prose*

Dante's Paradise: *A Retelling in Prose*

The Famous Victories of Henry V: *A Retelling*

From the Iliad *to the* Odyssey: *A Retelling in Prose of Quintus of Smyrna's* Posthomerica

George Chapman, Ben Jonson, and John Marston's Eastward Ho! *A Retelling*

George Peele's The Arraignment of Paris: *A Retelling*

George Peele's The Battle of Alcazar: *A Retelling*

George Peele's David and Bathsheba, and the Tragedy of Absalom: *A Retelling*

George Peele's Edward I: *A Retelling*

George Peele's The Old Wives' Tale: *A Retelling*

William Shakespeare's 38 Plays: Retellings in Prose
William Shakespeare's 1 Henry IV, aka Henry IV, Part 1: *A Retelling in Prose*
William Shakespeare's 2 Henry IV, aka Henry IV, Part 2: *A Retelling in Prose*
William Shakespeare's 1 Henry VI, aka Henry VI, Part 1: *A Retelling in Prose*
William Shakespeare's 2 Henry VI, aka Henry VI, Part 2: *A Retelling in Prose*
William Shakespeare's 3 Henry VI, aka Henry VI, Part 3: *A Retelling in Prose*
William Shakespeare's All's Well that Ends Well: *A Retelling in Prose*
William Shakespeare's Antony and Cleopatra: *A Retelling in Prose*
William Shakespeare's As You Like It: *A Retelling in Prose*
William Shakespeare's The Comedy of Errors: *A Retelling in Prose*
William Shakespeare's Coriolanus: *A Retelling in Prose*
William Shakespeare's Cymbeline: *A Retelling in Prose*
William Shakespeare's Hamlet: *A Retelling in Prose*
William Shakespeare's Henry V: *A Retelling in Prose*
William Shakespeare's Henry VIII: *A Retelling in Prose*
William Shakespeare's Julius Caesar: *A Retelling in Prose*
William Shakespeare's King John: *A Retelling in Prose*
William Shakespeare's King Lear: *A Retelling in Prose*
William Shakespeare's Love's Labor's Lost: *A Retelling in Prose*
William Shakespeare's Macbeth: *A Retelling in Prose*
William Shakespeare's Measure for Measure: *A Retelling in Prose*
William Shakespeare's The Merchant of Venice: *A Retelling in Prose*
William Shakespeare's The Merry Wives of Windsor: *A Retelling in Prose*
William Shakespeare's A Midsummer Night's Dream: *A Retelling in Prose*
William Shakespeare's Much Ado About Nothing: *A Retelling in Prose*
William Shakespeare's Othello: *A Retelling in Prose*
William Shakespeare's Pericles, Prince of Tyre: *A Retelling in Prose*
William Shakespeare's Richard II: *A Retelling in Prose*
William Shakespeare's Richard III: *A Retelling in Prose*
William Shakespeare's Romeo and Juliet: *A Retelling in Prose*
William Shakespeare's The Taming of the Shrew: *A Retelling in Prose*
William Shakespeare's The Tempest: *A Retelling in Prose*
William Shakespeare's Timon of Athens: *A Retelling in Prose*
William Shakespeare's Titus Andronicus: *A Retelling in Prose*
William Shakespeare's Troilus and Cressida: *A Retelling in Prose*
William Shakespeare's Twelfth Night: *A Retelling in Prose*
William Shakespeare's The Two Gentlemen of Verona: *A Retelling in Prose*
William Shakespeare's The Two Noble Kinsmen: *A Retelling in Prose*
William Shakespeare's The Winter's Tale: *A Retelling in Prose*